Dedication

I dedicate this book, to my dear friend, Barbara Rothenberg. She brings a constant source of happiness in my life just by her very presence. As long as Barbara is nearby, you will always find, if not on my face, a smile in my heart.

And to all those out there, both men and women, who fear they will never find true love, just remember, 'there's a lid for every pot.'

Acknowledgments

I can't go without expressing my thanks and support to the singular love and support of my husband, Paul. This incredible journey we call life, in my humble opinion, is significantly improved by the addition of someone special to share the journey with.

The Rescuer

By Eric Huffbind

M/M Gay Romance Novel

© Copyright 2017 by Eric Huffbind

The author can be reached at **eric@erichuffbind.com**.

Editors: Ann Attwood, Tanja Ongkiehong
Book Cover Artist: Jennifer Craig
ISBN-10: 1536813788
ISBN-13: 978-1536813784

Table of Contents

CHAPTER ONE
A New Beginning

This morning the summer sunlight streamed into Christopher's bedroom, waking him up out of what was a restless slumber. Having difficulty prying his eyes open, he immediately shaded them with his hands because of the blinding radiance streaming in through the window. He felt like absolute shit! Hungover was truly a better adjective to describe what he was experiencing. Unfortunately, this response to his use of alcohol had become far too familiar—and he'd had enough.

He gazed around the room only to be reminded that this was, in fact, not his bedroom. Instead, he recalled he was in a private room at the Watermeadow Rehabilitation and Recovery Center. "Oh jeez, how quickly I forgot that I checked myself in here yesterday," he said to himself aloud. The walls of the room were pale shades of blue and teal. There was a twin-size bed, a small couch, a dresser filled with drawer spaces, and a reclining chair with a built-in footrest. These complete blackouts of memory and time had happened with ever-increasing frequency.

His life had been spinning rapidly out of control and—quite frankly—he felt like he was now down in a very deep trough. He was low on cash and could no longer hold down a respectable job. He looked like absolute hell, and many of his friends were becoming distant. Who could blame them? Heck, he wouldn't wish to associate with others like himself. Recently, he'd reached twenty-seven years of age, and he knew, in his heart and soul, that he shouldn't be following this pathway. It wasn't what he wanted, nor was it what his parents wanted.

He hated disappointing his parents as far back as he could remember. Hell, it wasn't just his parents; if he was to be honest, he hated disappointing himself. Honesty with himself was a concept he knew he had to deal with, but he hadn't been doing such a bang-up job of it.

Growing up his entire life in Indianapolis, Indiana, he always tried to excel at everything he invested himself in. In the past, he'd met with significant success, always turning in report cards of straight As and the occasional B. During his childhood, his bedroom was filled with trophies and ribbons from every gymnastics event he participated in, spelling bees, science fairs, piano recitals, and any number of accomplishments. To this very date, his parents had not removed any of those symbols of success from what used to be his old bedroom. Nate and Maggie held onto those memories of their bright and talented son. He was proud of his successes and loved the limelight that was cast upon him every time he'd had some new achievement during his youth. Youth, however, was now a faraway, very distant memory.

He knew he was no dummy. Quite the opposite, he'd been gifted with keen intelligence and a strong aptitude for whatever he put his mind to. He learned new things quite easily. His parents hardly saw him crack a book during high school, but his grades never suffered. Not one bit; unlike his younger brother Jeremy, who struggled to get by. Jeremy would spend hours studying just to get a C. Their parents knew they shouldn't have favorites, but despite that, Christopher knew he'd been theirs. Not that they ever made such a statement, but it was obvious. What was there not to be proud of during those younger years?

The silence was suddenly broken by, "Good morning."

"Oh, dear God, you startled me!" Christopher exclaimed in a frightened voice.

"I'm terribly sorry! I didn't mean to scare you. My name is Judy. I'm one of the nurses here on the third floor. How are you feeling this morning?" Christopher sensed the kindness in her voice.

"Like a thousand jackhammers are going off in my head—and I can't find the power switch to shut them off. I've the worst splitting headache, and my stomach is so queasy; I feel like I could hurl at any moment. Gosh, other than that I'm just *peachy keen*."

"Well, it's nice to see you have a sense of humor about yourself. That's a positive. Although considering how incoherent you've been the past three days, you look quite good to me."

"Wait a minute, you mean I didn't arrive here yesterday?"

"I'm afraid not, sweetheart. You came in last Tuesday, the 13th. It's now Sunday, the 18th. After you'd gone forty-eight hours without alcohol, you slipped into…" Judy trailed off. "Medically speaking, it's called Delirium Tremens. That's just a medical term for alcohol withdrawal. Actually, it can be very deadly. We've given you Ativan—it's an anti-anxiety medication—roughly every six hours to keep you from injuring yourself or anyone else close to you while they were providing care. Sorry to tell you, but we had to keep you in wrist restraints until very early this morning. The night nurse said you finally started calming down, so he took them off. See there, still tied to the sides of your bed," Judy said as she pointed to the restraints.

"Oh man, I've really hit rock bottom, haven't I?"

"That's not for me to say," Judy replied. "Only you can answer whether you hit rock bottom or not. Still, if that's what you feel in your heart, acknowledging that very fact is an excellent way to begin the recovery process. Tell you what; I can bring you some Tylenol and Phenergan to ease the discomfort of your headache and nausea. Would you like that?"

"Yes, please, that's very kind. Could you also bring me some towels and bathing supplies so I can clean myself up? I'm sure I must be *awfully* ripe by now."

Judy smiled. "Sure thing. Be right back."

After taking the medications and resting several hours, Christopher finally felt some relief. He climbed out of bed, stripped off the hospital gown, and stepped into a hot shower. The steamy water cascading over his body felt like a warm embrace. While he lathered his body, he began to feel much more awake and coherent. His head was the clearest he'd experienced in a long time. After he toweled off, he slipped into a pair of blue jeans and a gray T-shirt he found in the dresser drawer. He did recall wearing them when he arrived at Watermeadow.

Looking in the mirror on the wall of his room, Christopher noticed a week-long growth of facial hair. "Eek! I look horrible with this scraggly beard," he said while running his fingertips over his cheeks and chin. Fortunately, he discovered he'd brought his favorite electric razor with him. He grabbed it from the dresser drawer and buzzed his face back down to his preferred, clean-shaven look. *Now, that's more like it.*

Just then he heard a knock on the door of his room. "Come in," he responded. "Oh, hi, Mom. Hi, Dad," he said nonchalantly.

"How are you feeling?" his mother asked.

"Actually, I feel pretty well."

"So glad to hear it. Better yet, I'm happy to see you up and about and not tied to that bed in that horrible delusional state you were in. I hated coming here and seeing you like that," she said sadly.

"You gave us a terrible fright, son," his father added.

"I'm sorry, guys. I know I've been a disappointment to you for a long time. Hell, I've been a disappointment to myself for that matter!"

"Honey, your mother and I just don't understand why you've allowed yourself to be consumed by alcohol," his father stated with great concern. "You were such a great kid growing up; always a winner! What happened?" Nate Parker raised his sons to be good, decent, and God-fearing people. Seeing his pride and joy like this just baffled him. It ate at his very soul.

"Guys, I can't talk about it with you right now," Christopher said.

"That's all we ever hear from you! That you can't talk about it!" Maggie Parker screeched. Realizing she'd broken her promise to herself, she continued more gently, "I'm sorry, sweetheart, I didn't mean to scream at you."

Christopher had buried a secret deep inside where no one could find it. He had locked it away, but during his twenties, the secret continued to eat away at him. Alcohol was just a tool he kept in his arsenal—the arsenal he relied on to dull the pain and disappointment in himself. During recent months, he'd slowly become aware of how alcohol abuse was endangering his life, which is why he felt he needed to seek professional guidance.

"Well, you're going to talk to someone here about what's been eating you. This rehab facility is costing your Mom and me a small fortune! We only want the best for you. You know that, don't you?"

"Yes, Dad, I know!" Christopher snapped back. "You've drilled that into me my whole life, about how much you've spent on Jeremy and me. Damn it, Dad! I think I've lived my entire life trying to please you and Mom. I'm so sorry I'm such a disappointment. I guess I'm not perfect after all." Tears began to well up in his eyes. Completely exhausted from trying to please his parents, a familiar sense of anxiety started to come over him—the same anxiety he'd camouflage by drinking. There wasn't any alcohol to reach for now. Christopher's eyes became too full to contain his tears as they coursed down his cheeks.

"You're upsetting him," interrupted his mother. "You promised me you weren't going to do that!"

"I apologize; I didn't want to get you all worked up. I just want what's best for you," his father said.

"I know, Dad, I know," Christopher replied rather unconvincingly.

"We love you so very much," his mother said.

"I know you do." Although deep down he felt their love was conditional, and in his mind, that didn't feel like true, sincere love.

Mr. and Mrs. Parker each gave their son a long hug. "Dry your tears, honey. We're sorry to have upset you. We'll just go and let you calm down," Christopher's mother said. And with that, his parents said their goodbyes and took their leave.

Christopher immediately grabbed some tissues from the top of the dresser and dried his tears; he then sat down on the edge of the bed and took in some deep, cleansing breaths, hoping for some calm to wash over him. What was to become of him now? He knew damn well he couldn't keep drinking away his troubles. However, he'd now spent so many years trying to numb the pain caused by his problems, he'd forgotten how to act in the real world.

CHAPTER TWO
Susan Rogers

"Sweetheart?" As the young woman eased her way through the door of Christopher's room, he knew right away it was his best friend, Susan.

"I'm so glad to see you," he sighed with relief. Susan Rogers was, without doubt, his closest and certainly most loyal friend. At this point, she was about his only friend. She'd put up with all his mental health and alcohol abuse issues. But even she was starting to reach the end of her tether.

They'd known each other since ninth grade. She didn't have the aptitude as Christopher, so frequently, she studied with him during those high school years, absorbing as much knowledge as she could. He'd *always* been there for her, and so the two bonded tightly. They became inseparable—always sharing their most intimate thoughts. She would do just about anything for him, if she felt it would help.

He bolted to her and threw his arms around her, hugging her as tightly as he could while sobbing, feeling frightened and alone. She was the only friend Christopher could truly be himself with.

"Honey, what's wrong? You've had me worried sick ever since you slipped into that horrible delusional state. Thank God! You look so much better now than when I brought you here. Why are you crying, honey?"

Trying to stop his tears, he blurted out, "I'm so ashamed of myself! I've become such an embarrassment to myself and my family. I don't know what I've done in life to deserve you, though. I can't thank you enough for coming."

His parents were crazy about Susan. She was a strong, intelligent, and beautiful woman. They always felt she was a great catch for their eldest son. Nate and Maggie simply could never figure out why their son was so dense not to see it for himself.

"Oh, I just love you so damn much; I always have. You're such perfect husband material," Susan said in a slightly sarcastic and playful tone. "I love your kindness, your warmth, your great sense of humor, and you're smart as a whip! Not to mention you're so damn cute with your dark-brown hair, emerald-green eyes, and a smile that could melt glaciers. You know how I enjoy getting lost in your eyes. Darn — you're just plain hot! Why did you have to go mess it all up by being gay?"

Christopher smiled and blushed, "Thanks. That's so sweet of you to say. You make everything sound so poetic. You're welcome to look into my eyes all you want. I'm glad you enjoy them so much." Deep down, he loved the flattery she showered on him. It always felt good that she found him attractive, and he was always much happier whenever she was present.

"I'm just honest," she laughed. "Let's sit down here," she said, pointing to the small couch in the room.

When they were sitting next to each other, Christopher said whimsically, "You would've been a perfect girlfriend, a great wife! Except for just one thing."

"And what's that?" she asked with a puzzled look.

"Ummm — I love dick!" he smirked.

"Oh yeah, there is *that*," she said in a drawn-out, snide tone.

"You deserve better than I could ever give you. You should be with a man who can give you the love and romance you deserve."

"Oh, sweetheart, you give me something very special—your friendship. That being said, I can't handle your drinking anymore. I just can't. As much as I love you, I've had it! You're killing me inside. I want to see you grow old and fall in love with a nice guy; get married even. You're going to kill yourself at this rate!"

"I know, I know," he repeated, staring down at the floor. "I'll give it up; I have to. I promise. That's all there is to it."

Susan choked up. "I don't want to live in a world without you here with me. You simply have to put your life back together!"

Wanting some comfort, he curled up on the couch, pressing the left side of his face into her bosom. That was her cue to wrap her arms around him and just hold on. Nothing else was required. She relished their cuddle sessions. It was the only time she felt their relationship could ever be *more than friends*.

"Wake up, honey, wake up," her voice suddenly aroused Christopher.

Now awake, he responded sleepily, "Gosh, I fell asleep on you—I'm sorry about that."

"That's okay, I didn't have the heart to wake you, but I've got to be going, sweetie."

"So soon?" he lamented, not wanting her to leave.

"Sweetheart, it's been two hours. The staff here brought your dinner a while ago. It's been sitting here waiting for you."

He unfolded himself off the couch, and they both stood up. He gave Susan a hug, squeezing hard. "Thank you for coming."

"Sure thing. Oh, I almost forgot." She reached into her purse, which she'd left sitting on the bed, and pulled out a cell phone. "Here—

I wanted you to have your phone back now that you look so much better. I've been holding onto it since that delirium set in. So, call me or text me. I want to know how you're doing."

Susan reached into a large shopping bag she'd brought. "I also stopped by your apartment on the way here to find you some changes of clothing."

"Oh, thank you so much. I don't know what I'd do without you. You're a godsend! You *will* be back, won't you?" he asked apprehensively.

"Of course, I'll be back, sweetheart. But I can't be here all the time. I do have to work sometimes, you know. I've a huge wedding coming up soon, with more than four hundred guests."

Susan was an event planner. She loved her work and was good at it. She'd managed to build up a nice set of clients over the past six years. And they all wanted to be taken care of and pampered.

She gave Christopher a peck on the lips. "I love you. Take care of yourself. We'll talk soon. Okay?"

"Okay, I love you, too. Bye. I'll miss you."

"Miss me? But honey, I'm only a phone call away," she responded reassuringly.

"Of course, you are. I just hate being alone right now."

"I understand how you feel, but I really must be leaving. Goodnight, love." With that, she picked up her purse, gave him another quick hug and left. She finally felt some comfort. At the very least, she felt Christopher was safe. That thought put a smile on her face as she walked back to her car in Watermeadow's parking lot.

Christopher ate his dinner and watched some television. By 10:30 that evening, he had grown very sleepy. He turned down his bed and crawled in for the night, not knowing what tomorrow would bring. As he closed his eyes, all he could do was hope and pray for the best.

CHAPTER THREE
Jason and Peter

It was 6:00 pm, Sunday evening when the doorbell rang. Jennifer called downstairs to her husband, Peter, "Honey, would you please get the door? It's probably Jason."

As predicted, Jason Calhoun was at the front door. "Hey there, good to see you. Please, come in, come in." Peter gave him a huge bear hug as he always did. Jennifer and Peter Berringer were Jason's closest friends. He'd often seek them out for companionship.

He was down in the dumps since he had broken up with yet another boyfriend. Jason, now thirty years of age, was so tired of being alone and was more than ready to find Mr. Right. However, he wasn't willing to settle. He was far too wise for that. He was a college-educated social worker and during his career had counseled many couples with failing marriages. There always seemed to be one common thread among all those couples: one of the spouses had *settled*. So, he was determined he was not going to settle on just anyone.

Peter offered Jason something to drink as they moved into the family room. "Oh, I'm fine for now," Jason replied. Jennifer had ventured down the stairs to see her most cherished friend from college.

"There's my favorite BFF!" she exclaimed.

"Your *favorite* BFF? You mean you have *more than one* BFF? How is that possible? I'm hurt. I should be your one and only BFF," Jason responded in a playful, yet sarcastic tone.

"So, sorry. Yes, you're my *only* BFF. I don't know how I could have made such a mistake. Come over here and give me a hug. Oh, it's so good to see you." The two embraced tightly. They'd met each other at the University of Indianapolis and had remained the best of friends.

"So, now what did Elliot do to make you break it off?"

"Elliot!" Jason exclaimed. "Elliot was the guy I dated before John," he said in a how-can-you-not-remember tone of voice.

"See, I told you he's been seeing a Daniel," Peter said.

"No, Daniel was like three boyfriends ago! Most recently, I was dating Phillip."

Jason Calhoun was a hardcore serial monogamist, always hunting for his Prince Charming—a relentless romantic to the core. Well, Prince Charming couldn't be found fast enough as far as he was concerned. He was ready to settle down with that perfect someone. He tried on men like shopping for new sweaters in autumn.

Jennifer and Peter now stood in the family room, feeling embarrassed. After all, they were his dearest friends, but they struggled to keep up with his on-again-off-again romances. They both loved him, and all they wanted was for him to meet the right guy.

Jason continued, "It's okay guys. I know I've been dating a constant string of men. I can see how confusing it is to keep up with all my relationships. Thank you, Peter, for coming out with me tonight. I sure didn't want to be alone this evening." Turning towards Jennifer, "I especially want to thank you, for letting me borrow your husband for the night—he'll have to suffice until I get one of my own," he laughed at himself.

"Oh, honey, you're welcome. I'm only sorry I couldn't join you. I just have so many papers I need to grade this evening," she said. Jennifer was an English teacher at the nearby Williamson High School.

17

"So, I'm more than happy to loan you my husband, just as long as you return him safely." She leaned over to give her husband a kiss on the lips. "Where are you going tonight?"

"We thought we would go downtown to the Hoosier Café for some burgers and beer," Peter replied. It was one of their favorite restaurants.

"Well, you two boys run along so I can get started with my grading." Jennifer motioned with her hands as if she was trying to scoot them out the door.

"Do you want to drive, or should I?" Jason asked.

"I can drive; be happy to."

They both smiled. "Well, we'll see you later, honey," Peter said to his wife.

Jennifer gave her husband one last kiss, "You boys have fun."

The two men got a table near a window and were both sitting in front of ice-cold beers. A waiter had already taken their order—they both ordered the Deluxe Indy Cheeseburger and fries—and were now waiting for their dinner to arrive. The Hoosier Café was a fun, hip restaurant decorated in an Art Deco style. Jason was staring into his beer while slowly spinning the glass as if in a deep trance. He looked as though his best friend had just died; he felt so despondent.

"Are you going to be okay?" Peter asked.

He sighed. "Oh, yes, I'm sure. What I want is to be a *Jennifer*."

"Huh? What on earth do you mean 'you want to be a *Jennifer*'?"

"Jennifer has someone to share her bed with at night. She's happily married to a great guy—that being you. That's why *I* want to be a *Jennifer*. I'm tired of being alone. I just don't know why it's so hard to meet a nice guy. I'm grateful I live in a country where two men *can* now legally get married. God knows, many members of the gay community never thought we'd ever see the day. I'd like to be able to take advantage of this new-found freedom."

"Buddy, I'm sorry you're having such a tough time. You just need to 'keep shaking the bushes.' Mr. Right has to be out there somewhere. I just know he is."

"Are you kidding me? Keep shaking the bushes? *You* keep shaking the bushes because I'm sick of the shit that keeps falling out of them."

With that, Peter let out a huge roar of laughter. He laughed so hard Jason couldn't help but start turning up the corners of his lips into a subtle smile. "Uh-oh, is that a smile I see? I think it is. Yes, that's *definitely* a smile," Peter teased. Now, Jason was grinning ear-to-ear. Peter was glad to finally see a smattering of happiness on his friend's face, even if only for a moment. "Gosh, I'm trying to remember. How long have you and Jennifer known each other?"

"Oh gee, let me think a second." Christopher replied, "Ummm, if I recall, we met in our sophomore year of college. Yeah, that was it."

"You know, I'm sort of embarrassed to tell you this. I never had any gay friends growing up. Not until Jennifer introduced me to you. To be honest, I think I was 'too macho' back in high school to have any gay friends. I was such a dick!"

"Well, I hope you're friends with me because I'm a nice guy, not because I'm gay," Jason responded diplomatically.

"Of course, of course. I didn't mean any disrespect. It's just that I feel like you've taught me a lot, or rather you've made me a better person. I'm ashamed of my prejudices during my youth. You mean a lot to me. I really do enjoy spending time with you."

"Awwwww, that's so sweet of you to say." Jason reached over to clasp the top of Peter's hand. "I feel very much the same. I was so happy for Jennifer when she met you. She found a great catch in finding you."

"Hey, I've kind of an embarrassing question to ask," Peter said, suddenly feeling shy.

"Sure. What's the question?"

"Well, I was curious." Peter was behaving very sheepish now. "Do you find me attractive?"

The biggest shit-eating grin crawled across Jason's face. "Oh, my God, you're going to embarrass *me*! One of the primary reasons your wife and I got along so well all those years ago is because we had the same taste in men," Jason laughed. "Here I am sitting with her husband, looking at him across the table with all that chest hair climbing out of the V of his shirt collar. It's a wonder I'm not popping a boner under the table."

"Oh, I see, so you love my chest hair—huh?" Peter teased in his cockiest voice. "Well, maybe I should just unbutton a couple more buttons over here." He playfully did just that.

"Good heavens! I can't believe you just did that." Jason blushed beet red. "Dear God, please don't tell your wife about this conversation. God forbid she ever thought I was ogling her husband. Now, please know how much I care about you both, and I'd *never* do anything to jeopardize that. I know my boundaries for heaven's sake!"

"Oh, please, don't be embarrassed." Jason knew real sincerity when he heard it and knew Peter was genuine. "I was only trying to cheer you up a bit. Still, I'm flattered you think I'm good looking. Since I never had a gay, close friend until you, I was—well—I was—just curious if a gay guy would think I was nice to look at." Peter shrugged his shoulders, "That's all."

"You're very nice to look at—trust me," Jason said. "You're what I'd call a guy who's very 'easy on the eyes'."

"Thank you. I appreciate the compliment. It's nice to hear. Oh, here, let me button up my shirt again. I guess I'm making a *silly fool* of myself."

Before Peter had a chance to reach up to refasten his shirt, Jason scolded him playfully. "Don't you dare! I might as well enjoy the eye candy from this side of the table." The two men roared with laughter.

"Here's your dinner, gentlemen. I hope you enjoy," said the waiter as he placed two plates of cheeseburgers and fries on the table.

"Thanks again for hanging out with me tonight. I feel a whole lot better now than when we got here."

"Good. I'm glad to hear it," Peter said with a smile. "Look—I know how much you want to meet that special someone, but don't lose faith. I promise you he's out there somewhere. Maybe you should take a break for a while—don't try so hard. Someone wise once told me 'the right person will show up when you least expect it'."

"Hmmm, and who was that smart person?" asked Jason.

"If memory serves me right, that smart person was *you*."

He grumbled back, "Sure sounds like something I'd say. But I'm starting to doubt myself. Is there a Mr. Right for me? I don't feel like I'm all that picky. All I want is a cute guy with beautiful eyes, who doesn't smoke or drink too much, doesn't abuse drugs, votes Democratic, good solid job, isn't drowning in debt, not a closet case, and…" Jason's voice trailed off.

"And what?" Peter inquired.

Jason closed his eyes, trying to draw a vision with his mind's eye. Speaking in a wishful tone, "and a dark, five o'clock shadow across his face, broad shoulders, about six-feet tall, and a muscular chest and abs covered in dark hair."

"Oh, is *that* all you want?"

"Well, a guy can always dream, can't he?"

"Certainly," Peter said with emphasis. "What is that old saying I've always heard you say about finding the right person?"

"There's a lid for every pot," both men said in unison, laughing.

"Okay, I'll stop trying so hard for now, but I'm still praying a lid tumbles out of a kitchen cabinet very soon."

CHAPTER FOUR
The Social Worker

C hristopher was eating breakfast the next morning in the rehab center's main dining room. It was relatively small, with about seven rectangular tables. The décor of the rehab facility had a contemporary design and furnishings in pastel blues and grays, which appealed to his sense of style. Watermeadow allowed patients the option of eating in their private rooms if they preferred.

Off from the right side, a gentleman approached to offer his greetings. Christopher froze up—as far as he was concerned, this man was devastatingly handsome! Drop—dead—gorgeous! The most beautiful creature he'd ever laid eyes on in all his twenty-seven years: dark ash-brown hair, piercing brown eyes, a sweet smile, a tapered waistline, and sort of a nerdy *Clark Kent* look. He worshiped men who gave off a nerdy vibe, and he couldn't take his eyes off this one.

"Excuse me, Mr. Parker, I believe?" asked the stranger while extending his right hand.

Accepting the stranger's hand, "Yes, that's me. My name is Christopher Parker. Uh... umm... I'm—very pleased—to meet you," he stammered. "How did you know it was me?" He was a tad confused. "Or rather, how did you know my name? I'm not even in my room."

"When you were admitted, we took a picture of you, and it's now part of your records here. That way, if you're not in your room, and roaming somewhere in our facility, one of the staff can recognize you. Plus, Judy—your nurse—was kind enough to point you out. So, I had a slight advantage. Anyhow, my name is Jason—Jason Calhoun. I'm a licensed clinical social worker and your case manager. I specialize in chemical dependency, and my role is to help in your recovery process. That's, of course, if you're willing to accept my help. My office is just down the hall in room 318," he said while gesturing with a pointed index finger. "I was hoping we could meet and talk this morning at 10:30 perhaps."

"Uh… Sure, that sounds great. Room 318 at 10:30. I'll be there."

"Great, well, I'm looking forward to getting to know you better. I'll let you finish your breakfast. See you then." The social worker turned away and took his leave.

Just that quickly, Christopher felt an erection creeping up in his khakis. *Fuck! How on earth am I ever going to focus on my recovery while looking at that man across a room. Although a little eye candy can't hurt,* he thought to himself silently trying to regain his composure. *Okay now, just cool your jets. Jason is just a nice guy, who's here to help you get your life back in order. But who just happens to be more beautiful than a Hawaiian sunset over the Pacific Ocean.* He took a deep breath and exhaled.

He went ahead and finished his breakfast and walked back to his private room. He then grabbed his cell phone, which he'd left on a bed-side table. He just had to send out a quick text to the one person who actually gave a shit about him.

Christopher: Hey there, I just met my social worker and case manager here. He's the most beautiful thing on two legs I've ever seen. He's sooooooo cute.

Susan: You better be on your best behavior, then! Don't even think about making a move on him. Remember, he's a professional there for your rehab. Please, I want you to get better.

Christopher: Yes, I know. I'll behave. Still, he's very nice to look at. Besides, he's probably straight anyway. It's not like I'd ever have a chance.

Susan: Please, I'm begging you. I want you to get well. I mean what I'm saying. Sweetie, I'm meeting a client in fifteen minutes. I need to run. Love you.

Christopher: Okay, I promise, I'll behave. Love you too.

Jason heard a knock on his office door. He stood up to open it immediately. "Hi there—welcome. Thank you for being on time. Please come in and have a seat. I want you to be completely comfortable here."

Christopher took a seat on a small couch in his office making sure he was behaving respectful of the invitation. The colors and décor were very much in keeping with the rest of the Watermeadow facility. "How should I address you? Mr. Calhoun?"

"You don't need to be formal; you can simply address me by my first name, Jason, and I'll call you, Christopher, if that's okay with you?"

"That's fine with me."

"Great. Somehow, I feel being on a first name basis makes my patients feel more at ease. I value your comfort. I want you to be able to speak freely in here. So, I was just looking over your records and from what I can tell, you were detoxing in the unit here for about three days.

You appear to have recovered quite well now—you look good. Excellent actually. How are you feeling, physically speaking?"

"I feel just fine. Never better."

"That's good. That means the worst part of your recovery is over. Now the fun begins."

"The fun? What fun? I must be missing something because I've yet to have a good time," he said with a smile yet a slight sneer in the delivery.

"Look—I know this isn't where you—or any patient for that matter, want to be. But if I'm not mistaken, based on your records, it appears it was your choice to admit yourself. I have to assume you wish to become sober of your own free will. Is that not the case?"

Responding in his most articulate way, "It most definitely is the case! I'm sick and tired of being—sick and tired. I'm tired of the blackouts. I've had enough of feeling horrible hangovers every morning, and the only thing that'll help is more alcohol. I also know if I don't stop this perpetual—self-destruction, I'm more than likely to wind up dead. It's just that simple."

"Wow! You're quite impressive. It usually takes days or weeks of therapy before most patients come to this conclusion. That's really quite remarkable."

"What can I say—I'm kind of smart," Christopher said in a rather shy-sheepish tone.

Jason laughed, "That's humble of you to admit."

"Honestly, I'm not trying to be arrogant."

"No, I can sense you're a very intelligent man."

Christopher thought to himself, *Gosh, can you sense my rising libido from the beautiful view on this side of the room?* "Well, thank you," he said wearing a quirky smile.

"So then, being that you're such an intelligent guy…"

Cutting him off before he could continue, "Why am I so stupid as to drink myself into oblivion? Is that what you were going to ask?"

"Ummm—well—yes, why are you? Generally, I've found most individuals abusing drugs or alcohol are trying to protect themselves from other issues that—are not being dealt with appropriately. In other words, they are trying to avoid something that's painful. The alcohol is acting as a camouflage or rather a coping mechanism for some issue or issues that perhaps cause high anxiety. Does this sound like a possibility?"

Just then, Christopher's skin tone went white, as if every drop of blood in his body rushed to his inner core. His face became expressionless, his eyes glazed over, and he stared at the floor. Fear and apprehension gripped him like a strong vise.

"Hey, are you okay?" Jason asked with grave concern. Christopher nodded his head up and down in a slowly defined manner. "Something I've said upset you?" His patient's eyes welled up with tears. Jason reached over and took his right hand and held it. "Please let me help you. As bright as you are, I can sense there is some crisis or family problem that you don't quite know how to deal with, and I'm guessing alcohol was being used to ease the pain of it."

Christopher continued to remain dead silent. So, Jason reached over with his other hand, sandwiching Christopher's hand between both of his own. Christopher felt so panicked inside, he couldn't speak a word. Besides Susan, he'd never told a living soul he was gay. Now, of course, he never had to announce his sexuality to the men he had sex with. Those sexual partners could have cared less about him and how he identified his sexual orientation. But he had never come out to anyone of real importance to him. Not his parents, brother, relatives, or friends. There was only the one exception, Susan. She was the only one he ever confided in. The only one he trusted with that knowledge.

Jason asked, "Just take some deep breaths in and out. Will you do that for me?" Christopher nodded again and took slow, deep breaths. In and out, in and out, in and out. His face began to take on some color at last, albeit pale pink. "Are you in some sort of trouble? Have you committed some kind of crime?"

"No," Christopher finally spoke quietly.

Thank God, Jason internalized, *I finally got him to say something, even if it's a single syllable.* "Good, that's good, you haven't committed a crime. Listen—if you can tell me what's troubling you, we can try to work on a fix for it. A resolution of some kind. But I need you to talk to me. Whatever it is, I can handle it. I'm here to help you. Have you told any other person about this issue before?"

"One person," he nodded.

Okay, now I have two words and three syllables. That's progress. Shit, I'll take what I can get. "So, then you've trusted this information to someone else. That's good to hear. Please—believe me, I won't share this with anyone unless you authorize it." By now Christopher had tears spilling down his face. Jason, letting go of his hand, grabbed a box of tissues from his desk and placed it on a small table adjacent to them. "I truly want to help you—but you need to let me in."

Christopher took a tissue, wiped away his tears, and took another deep breath. "I don't think my problem is something that can be fixed," at last getting out a complete sentence.

"Go on. Hey look, if you haven't killed anyone or committed any crime, nothing can be *that* bad. What can't be fixed?"

The gaze of his eyes looked up and across to Jason's eyes, and he said with a catch in his voice, "I'm—gay. I'm sure you can't fix that. God knows I've wanted to."

"So, being gay is what has you so upset?"

"Yes. That's—part of it."

"Well, you're right—no, I can't fix that. And besides, I wouldn't want to. It's who you are. It's—it's like your green eyes. It is all part of what makes you—you. By the way, has anyone ever said you have an amazing eye color? They're a remarkable shade of green. Quite striking!"

He smiled bashfully. "Yes, I've been told that before. My father told me I had a great-grandmother who had the same green eyes. My father's grandmother who died *well* before I was born." He never forgot about those green eyes though. Sensing a sincere warmth and kindness from his new therapist, that Jason wasn't just beautiful to look at, but a man with a genuinely caring heart, and that brought a smile to his face.

"Well, look at that, I got a smile out of you. So, see—you wouldn't want to change the color of your eyes, would you?"

"No, I wouldn't," Christopher continued to smile.

"Likewise—I wouldn't want you to change your sexuality for me, nor should anyone else ask you to. Now, that being said, I'm not naïve," he said in a very matter of fact way. "I understand that being gay has its challenges. I know there are many in society—many in this world—who would rather you weren't gay. Now, taking a super wild ass guess here, I'm assuming that some individual or individuals in your life would rather you *not* be gay."

"Yep," he smirked back. "My dad. Not sure whether or not my mom would be bothered."

"Is your dad the one person you told?"

"Oh, God no!"

"Well then, how do you know it's going to upset him?"

"Trust me, I know," Jason firmly said.

"Did something happen that alerted you to the belief your father wouldn't accept you?"

"Yes. It was something that happened a long time ago." Trying to recall the hurtful memories from his past, anxiety slammed over Christopher. "I'm feeling very nervous right now. I just don't feel well at all." All this repressed emotional pain and anxiety was overflowing like water over a dam. For several years he didn't have to deal with these issues, since the alcohol dulled his emotional pain.

"Tell you what, we'll stop for the day. I'll ask your nurse to bring you some Ativan to help ease your nervousness. Okay—so, you go and rest. How about we meet again on Wednesday at 10:30. How does that sound?"

"Sure—I think I'd like that." Jason knew that he needed to participate for his rehabilitation to be successful. Otherwise, what was the point of him being there. Plus—he still enjoyed the eye candy despite the emotional roller coaster. He stood up and being gracious, he shook Jason's hand and told him, "Thank you." Then he left the office.

CHAPTER FIVE
Samuel Barron

Christopher made his way back to his room to wait for Judy to arrive with his anxiety medication. Seated and restlessly waiting, he stared out his window looking for some calm to consume him. When Judy arrived with his medication twelve minutes later, he wasted no time, grabbing the small cup and immediately swallowing the Ativan washing them down with a long drink of water. Forcing himself to lie down, he tried desperately to relax.

He grabbed his smartphone thinking he could flip on some light classical music. That had always helped him to relax in the past. He'd become so accustomed to resolving his panic with alcohol, but now, that solution was clearly not a possibility. He had to get off this frightening merry-go-round of solving all his problems that way. How was he going to manage without his familiar friend? Forty-five minutes later, he was out like a light. Peace washing over him at last.

Feeling a set of lips gently pressing on his forehead, Christopher woke up to someone kissing him. He found a strange man gazing down on him; his eyes weren't quite in focus yet.

"How are you feeling?" asked the stranger.

Christopher suddenly sprang up from the bed recognizing in a split second whose voice it was. "Sam! What the fuck are you doing here?" Eyes now focusing at one-hundred percent.

"I was just checking in on you. I wanted to know how you were feeling? Can't a friend pay a visit?"

It was Samuel Barron or "Sam" as his cohorts called him. He was a powerful CEO of one of the nation's top five-hundred corporations, namely Viatone. They were makers of pharmaceuticals. In the years Christopher had known Sam, Viatone had grown to a five-hundred-billion-dollar company.

Sam was a bit more than just a CEO of a huge corporation. At one time, he was one of the nation's most eligible bachelors—a gorgeous hunk of a man to feast your eyes upon, despite his advancing years. His looks held up like a fine bottle of wine. Women all over the country would swoon over every magazine photo, television news spot, and social media post. And it wasn't just the women. Every gay man's dick would jump into action each time they saw an image of this man; Christopher had been among that crowd.

Mr. Barron exuded pure charisma everywhere he went and in everything he touched. *He'd been* one of the nation's most eligible bachelors. However, that status changed five years ago, when he married Patsy Rossmiller.

"You're *no* friend!" Christopher shouted back in his most snide and angry voice. "And you're not welcome here, you motherfucking son-of-a-bitch! Get the fuck out of my room! Better yet, get the hell out of my life!" He made no attempt to hide his feelings. Clearly, he was overwhelmed with upset; downright hostile and belligerent.

"Sweetheart, I've been worried sick about you," Sam said.

"I'm *not* your sweetheart. Not now—not ever," Christopher shouted with increasing volume. "You're not worried about me—you selfish asshole. You're concerned about your reputation. What would this country think of you if they knew the truth? The country—hell, what would the *world* think if they found out. That's all you care about. That's all you *ever* cared about."

"Look, you're not the only one who's in a position of power, and you know it!" The bastard CEO snarled back.

That was one comment Christopher did *not* want to hear, and it was the last straw. He couldn't take the presence of this man, not a single second more. He burst into tears yet again all the while he screamed as loud as he could.

"Get out! Get out! Get out! Get out!" Over and over, he yelled with increasing intensity. In no time at all, the third-floor staff came racing into Christopher's room; including Jason. Nurse Judy immediately saw the presence of Sam Barron, as did everyone else. She didn't have the slightest idea what was upsetting her patient to result in such a tumultuous reaction. Looking directly at the unwanted visitor, she calmly said, "Mr. Barron, I think you had better leave."

It wasn't as if she or anyone needed to be introduced to this man. Who wouldn't recognize him? Sam Barron's notoriety spread everywhere, particularly in the healthcare community. *But what the fuck is this man doing in Christopher Parker's room at Watermeadow of all places* was crawling through Jason's head. He just couldn't understand what their connection would be.

Mr. Barron knew he was outnumbered, so he nodded graciously and left as instructed. Christopher shouted after him, "And don't come back—ever! I never want to see you again!"

He now dissolved into a puddle of tears. Eying Jason from across the room, Christopher ran over and flung his arms around the man, weeping uncontrollably; desperately needing to be in the arms of a friend. And although his new case manager wasn't precisely a friend, he somehow knew he wouldn't be rejected. His weight, having grabbed Jason so suddenly, pulled them both tumbling to the floor.

Trying to calm him down with a soft, "shhhhhh, listen to me, if you don't want Mr. Barron coming back again, I can have him barred from the facility, at least while you're staying with us." The loud sobbing continued on Jason's shoulder. "Would you like that?"

Christopher replied in a faint whisper, "Yes, please."

Holding onto him tightly, he delivered a telling nod over to Judy. It was evident Christopher was overpowered with anger and anxiety that even the Ativan couldn't assist with. In a complete state of bewilderment, she indicated she would call security at once, preventing the return of this apparent nemesis. Jason was also just as bewildered as he looked over towards her. Despite Sam Barron's status in this world, he'd be damned if the man would interfere with a patient's recovery. He was a tremendous advocate where his patients were concerned. "You just cry as much as you need to."

Christopher tightened his grip around him even more while continuing to soak Jason's dress shirt with tears. But Jason didn't mind being clutched so tightly. It made him feel whole inside; that his life had meaning and purpose. It's what he was good at—being there for others when they needed him. He treasured being needed; he always did.

Unfortunately, he had learned that being needed, or rather *rescuing* others, didn't make for a good combination when it came to romance and love. It often led to the downfall of his romantic relationships with other men. He finally realized a romantic interest had to be emotionally, mentally, and financially stable. Now, he knew, there had to be some physical attraction. But the men he seemed to go for were all emotional train wrecks. So, why did he go for those guys? Because they needed him, and he had an unceasing craving for being needed. It was his life's purpose, or so he thought.

After ten minutes of constant sobbing, Christopher finally calmed down. The ongoing sniveling had quelled. Jason eased him off the floor and back into bed. "Lie down and rest for a while. Are you feeling better now?" He received a nod back that indicated a positive answer. So, Jason brought Christopher's feet up onto the bed and pulled the blanket across him. In his experience, a huge crying jag was exhausting.

Jason shut off the lights in the room and closed the door as he exited. He had a stack of paperwork sitting in his office, which needed his attention. One thing was certain in his mind, there weren't going to be any elves coming around to take care of it for him.

CHAPTER SIX
Jennifer Berringer

Jason was home for the evening in his north side Indianapolis condominium. His home was an industrial loft style unit, with exposed brick walls and aluminum HVAC ductwork that ran across the ceilings. The floors and countertops were made of smooth-surfaced concrete. A kitchen, well equipped with high-end appliances, and a contemporary glass tile, splash back providing a modern touch. He had placed several large area rugs in each room throughout the unit to give them a more cohesive feel—at least that's how he saw it. Many shades of blue were used as he most decidedly had a love affair with that color. His taste in furnishings was on the eclectic side, never deciding on a distinct style. Still, he had an excellent eye for aesthetics overall.

Jason had brought home some carryout pizza, which he simply loved. He was always up for a great slice, any time of day or night, the kind of guy who would be happy with cold pizza for breakfast. He never seemed to tire of it.

He'd perched himself on the edge of his couch watching television when his phone rang. He reached over to pick up, "Hello."

Jennifer was on the other end of the line. "Hey, sweetheart, I was just checking in to see how you are feeling this evening?"

"Much, much better actually. Your husband cheered me up quite a bit last night."

"I'm so glad to hear it. So...," she trailed off. "Anything exciting at work today?"

"Gee, I'll say there was," he said in a rather pleasant but stern tone.

"Oh really, so tell me, what happened?"

"Gosh, I really shouldn't say—you know with HIPAA laws, I can't divulge patient issues." Jason was secretly *dying* to tell her all about the day's events, specifically Sam Barron's odd appearance. The two of them both loved their fair share of gossip.

"You don't have to use any names," she said.

"Well, that's just it; I'm dying to talk about a particular person, and it's killing me that I just can't. Although this person isn't one of our patients. He's just a distinguished visitor who showed up to visit one of my new patients, who happens to be a recovering alcoholic. And I must say, I think he is the most beautiful green-eyed male specimen I've ever laid eyes on, *and* he's gay. Apparently, it's one of the reasons he's been drinking so heavily. Damn it," he sighed. "Why are the beautiful ones always so fucked up."

"Really?" she asked. "I never thought the fucked-up ones were all that nice to look at."

"Well—actually—you're right. Most of the heavy substance abusers aren't so 'easy on the eyes.' He's young still, so I suppose youth is playing in his favor. However, this guy is different somehow. He's bright, intelligent and *quite attractive,* if I must say."

"Apparently, you must," she quipped back. "He must be some looker. You didn't try to make a move on this guy? Did you?"

"Oh, dear God, of course not. I'd never behave in such an unprofessional manner. I've my license to think about, you know. Still—it's not as if I'm blind. I still appreciate a good-looking man when I see one. I mean—just because you're married doesn't mean you don't admire a sexy guy when you see one. Peter may not think you're looking, but I know you better than that. I know you *far* too well!"

"My husband isn't so naïve, I can assure you. Every time we go to a Bradley Cooper film, I'm swooning."

"Shit, Bradley Cooper, I'd be swooning too. Now getting back to the new patient I started with today, like I said, he's very bright and…" Jason had trouble finishing his sentence. "He has this very sweet, gentle nature about him. He strikes me as special. It's hard to put my finger on it. Somehow—he's different from other patients I've had rehabbing from alcohol abuse. I know how strange this sounds."

"The guy must have some kind of issues, though. At least that's what you've taught me about the psyche of this population. Don't let yourself be blinded by his beauty."

"No, you're most definitely correct on that point. This patient does, most definitely, have issues. What they all are—I don't know yet. He had a couple of big emotional meltdowns today."

Jennifer began to laugh, "Perhaps you can turn him into perfect husband material for yourself."

Jason sighed, "At the very least, I'd just like to help him become a great husband for someone. It won't be me, though. No thanks! I'd never dream of getting involved with a patient. It's just not appropriate. You know that of course. And, I never have success mixing romance with rescuing people from self-destruction. I always end up with my heart being broken."

"Yes, you've mentioned that to me before," Jennifer said in a somber tone.

"Okay, I'm not going down this rabbit hole of self-pity tonight. Hey, listen, I'm starving, and I've a sausage and mushroom pizza staring at me from my coffee table. Thanks so much for calling. I do love you. Oh, and would you give my love and thanks again to Peter for me."

"Will do. I love you too. Take care and have a good night."

Jason wasted no time getting back to his dinner after he hung up the phone. He was downright ravenous by this point. *If nothing else, I can drown my loneliness in pizza.* And with that thought, he took a bite and relished it.

CHAPTER SEVEN
Therapy Continues

It was Wednesday morning, and Christopher showed up at Jason's office as scheduled. The door was open as it often was. In his role as a counselor, Jason believed in having an open-door policy, and he tried his best to keep that promise to his patients. If the door was closed, his patients knew he was most probably working with a patient and privacy was required.

"Good morning," Jason greeted in his usual, cheerful manner. "Please come in—have a seat." Sitting down on the small couch, Christopher did his very best to keep a smile on his face, but underneath, he was somewhat apprehensive. Jason suspected that this patient had some deep emotional scarring to face, which the years had left behind. Although only twenty-seven years old, Christopher had insulated himself with invisible stone walls, always sheltering himself from self-disappointment. Many layers of his protective mask needed to be peeled off.

"Good—Good morning, Jason—you did say it was all right to address you that way, right?" he asked in a slightly stumbled, nervous fashion.

"Yes, that's just fine. Please—don't be nervous. My office should be a safe place for you. You seem a bit jittery. So please, just try and

39

relax. Take some deep breaths if you need to. You want to tell me what is making you—timid perhaps?"

Christopher took three deep breaths and finally let out a deep heavy sigh. "I suppose—I'm a bit embarrassed about throwing myself at you the other day, when I was sobbing."

"Nothing to be embarrassed over. I told you I am here to help you, and I meant every word of it. If you ever need a shoulder to cry on, I'm glad I can be here for you. Honestly, it's okay."

"If I'm going to be completely honest, my embarrassment is because…" But Christopher was feeling sheepish and found it difficult to complete his sentence.

"Because of what? You can tell me absolutely anything. You've no reason to be ashamed," Jason said, trying to be as reassuring as possible.

"But this is so embarrassing." Christopher couldn't believe he was going to admit this. "Because—I think—you're *really* cute, and here I was, throwing myself at you."

Jason felt himself blush briefly. "Thank you; that's very kind of you to say. Don't be embarrassed. It wasn't as if you were throwing yourself at me sexually. You were extremely upset."

"So, you don't think I'm just a huge—horndog?" Christopher asked with a lot of trepidation in his voice.

Jason waved a dismissive hand, "No. I think you're human, just like every other person on this planet. It's not a crime to be human. *And* it's not a crime to be gay. Well—at least not in the United States and many other countries." He felt he needed to interject that point, since he knew it was illegal to be gay in quite a number of countries. "Tell me, why were you crying so much. It was rather apparent you were not happy to see Sam Barron in your room."

Snapping back with disgust, "Sam Barron is a fucking asshole!" Suddenly, becoming aware of the obscenities, "I'm so sorry. I apologize for my bad language."

"Well, my door is closed, so it's only me who's hearing it. However, yes, let's try to keep the language here at Watermeadow at least PG rated. Although I've heard much worse than that. You want to explain to me why he upsets you so vehemently?"

"Not really. I hate the man with a passion. Believe it or not, I used to be in love with him. Or at the very least, I think I convinced myself I was in love." Christopher took another deep breath and let it out slowly. "I don't want to talk about that man—at least, I'm just not ready to."

Thoughts went racing through Jason's head suddenly. In love with him! What was going on between those two? And such a well-known figure. He's married to a woman. The guy is heterosexual. Isn't he? "Hey look, it's none of my business. We don't have to talk about him if you don't wish to. You mentioned on Monday you knew your father wouldn't accept you as a gay man. Can we talk about that? I think it's probably the most important."

"It started during my childhood. Growing up, I was the apple of my father's eye. I loved my dad so much, and he was like my very best friend. I was aware of being bright and smarter than my peers. I succeeded in everything I put my mind to. My old bedroom at my parents' is still covered with all my trophies, ribbons, awards, and all my successes. I was so proud of my accomplishments. I knew things came easier to me than to others, including my brother, Jeremy. I started developing feelings for other boys. I was like, thirteen-years-old at the time, when I noticed these strong attractions for other guys."

"Well, there's nothing wrong with being proud of your accomplishments and successes," Jason responded. "However, what led you to believe your dad was homophobic?"

Taking in another deep, cleansing breath and exhaling slowly, Christopher recalled, "I can still see the whole ugly scene play out in my head. When I was fifteen-years old, I had a good friend; his name was Richard Hoffman. We hung out a lot together. My parents liked the guy, and our parents were good friends at that time. That's how we met. Richard and I talked about everything. I felt like I could tell him anything. I could absolutely just be myself. I know he felt the same way towards me. We just clicked. It's not easy to find *true* friends in this world." Christopher paused.

"No, you're right, it's not easy to find *true* friends," Jason said with strong emphasis. "Someone for whom you can completely let your guard down. A friend who you can be completely honest with. Be your *true* self. It sounds like Richard was a very special friend."

"He was—how should I say this—a bit curious about other men sexually, like I was. I'm pretty sure he was gay as well. I suppose that may have been an influencing factor in why we clicked."

"I see," nodding to indicate a positive understanding.

"He was over at my house one day in my bedroom. We were studying for a biology test, I recall. Anyhow, I reached over and held onto his hand. I don't know why," wrinkling his brow, Christopher continued. "I just felt like it. I guess, as best as I can say, I had these romantic feelings towards him. Like a high school crush."

"Did you share these feelings you were having for Richard with your father or your mother even."

"God, no! You see, my father raised my brother and me to be God-fearing religious followers. I knew how he felt about homosexuals. I knew what the church thought."

"I see. So, in other words, you already had a sense that your father and perhaps your mother too, wouldn't be happy if they were to learn they had a gay son. Does that sound—about right?"

Now, getting a case of cotton mouth, Christopher asked for a glass of water. A bottle of water was immediately fetched from a small refrigerator in Jason's office. "Here you go. Please— go on with your story."

Christopher took a big swig from the water bottle. "Like I was saying, I was holding his hand while we were studying. And just holding his hand was enough to give me an erection. Then I noticed the swelling in his pants; it was apparent to me that he'd also gotten one. So, I reached over with my other hand and started massaging his penis through his pants. And—well—he returned the favor, I guess I'd say, and then one thing led to another. We began kissing. I mean *really* kissing, open mouths, tongues intertwining. You get the picture. That was my first experience. We got so involved with our," trying to be delicate, "heavy petting, I completely forgot I had left my bedroom door wide open."

"Ouch," Jason gasped. "Oh, no, you left the door open and let me guess. Your father walked by and saw what you and Richard were doing. Is that what happened?"

Almost in an instant, his eyes filled up with tears. "Yes. I've never seen so much anger in my father's eyes. I swear he turned three shades of purple, he was filled with so much rage. I somehow suspect my parents already had suspicions of me being gay. If they did, I assume what he saw confirmed their worst fears. He asked Richard to leave our home at once. He bolted as fast as his legs could carry him. My father scowled at me, told me he wasn't going to tell my mother, and I'd better not tell her either. He wanted to forget the image of what he had just witnessed, and he made it quite clear that he wouldn't accept me for who I was. For the man I was becoming. I was a gay adolescent, and my father wasn't going to have a *fag* for a son. He never wanted to talk about it ever again. We never have. Not in all these years."

"So—does your—father know you're gay?" Jason asked in a tottered fashion.

Christopher grabbed some tissues to blot away the tears streaming down his face. "I don't know what he believes anymore. We've never talked about that day again. He couldn't even bring himself to use the word *gay*."

"What about Richard? Do you still speak with him after all these years?"

"That's just it! I can't talk to him. When he left our house that day, Richard walked straight back to his house. Once he got there, he apparently knew where his father kept a revolver. His father had a home office and stored a gun in a desk drawer."

Jason's facial expression paled and glazed over with a look of horror and astonishment. "Oh, my God! I don't like where this is going."

"You said you wanted the truth, didn't you?" Christopher asked in an isn't-that-what-you-wanted voice.

"Yes, of course, please go on. I want you to be honest. So, what happened next?"

Christopher's vision blurred from his tears, and his face was tortured with anguish. "He placed the revolver to his head and pulled the trigger. Died instantly, at least, so he didn't suffer. His parents came home to find their only son lying in a pool of blood. I'm sure his parents never really understood why their son took his own life. Apparently, he must have been afraid my father would talk to his dad. As I said, my parents were close friends with his parents at the time. I honestly don't think my father would've said anything; he just wanted to block out the whole episode."

In all his time as a social worker, Jason had never experienced such a traumatic story from one of his patients. He was dumbfounded. "So, then these romantic feelings you had for this boy came to a sudden halt. Oh, heavens, this must have been devastating! You must have been grief-stricken. I can only assume how difficult it was for you!"

"I feel entirely responsible for his death. I've been racked with guilt ever since. I went numb inside. Like someone had shot me up with Novocain. I've never experienced anything like it before, or since."

"Please listen to me carefully. You're *not* responsible for his death. You hadn't intended to make out with him. You had no idea Richard would take his own life. You hadn't intended to be caught. Did you pull that trigger? Richard, himself, pulled the trigger. It was *his* choice, even if it was a poor choice. For God's sake, you were only fifteen-year-old boys. You were just a kid."

Now Christopher dissolved into tears, weeping uncontrollably. Hopping over to the small couch where his anguished patient sat, Jason pulled him into his right shoulder. Christopher just continued to bawl. Holding on to him, Jason knew these emotions had been bottled up for a very long time. At long last, Christopher could get these feelings out. After five minutes or so, he relaxed, and his tears ceased.

Soon Jason enquired, "How are you feeling?"

"Actually, much better now. You know, I've never shared that story with anyone. I feel like so much has been lifted off me now." Christopher responded shakily, "Like I was carrying the whole weight of the world on my shoulders. I feel so much lighter."

"Good, I'm glad." Starting to relax his grip on Christopher's shoulder. "You mentioned before there is already one person who knows you're gay."

"Yes, my friend Susan. We've been close friends since high school."

"Does she know about the suicide?"

"Nope, I never told her about it. Yes, she knew of my friendship with Richard, but I didn't tell her about the nature of our relationship. I never shared anything about us being caught by my father. Like I said, I went numb inside. I couldn't bring myself to tell anyone, not even Susan. I didn't disclose to her that I was gay till after high school. Susan wanted more from me than I could give her. And I loved her so much, I felt she had the right to know the truth about my sexuality. I could *never* be the boyfriend she wanted."

"That was honest of you. You were a good friend to her. As for the numbness, that makes sense to me."

"How so?" Christopher asked.

"When people experience the loss of a loved one, someone who held a very deep place in their heart, the immense grief you experienced, many individuals describe as going numb inside. *Especially* when the death comes suddenly and without warning. It sounds like you were in love with Richard. He gave you something at the time that only he could. He allowed you to be yourself. Your *real* self. Even if what you were—was a gay teenager. With him, you felt no shame for being—just you. You didn't have to experience the shame I suspect you felt inside with your father. Do your parents know your friend Susan?"

"Yes, they most certainly do. Like I said, we've been friends since high school. The best of friends. My parents are crazy about her. I think my father particularly liked her because she represented a female interest. Deep down, I sense my parents always wished our relationship would become something more than just friends. Like she was some bright shining hope; a person who could help my dad block out the memory of what he witnessed in my bedroom."

Nodding back, "Yes, that makes perfect sense to me as well. Gee, you're one intelligent guy. You know, I don't feel you had an opportunity to grieve properly for your loss. It was such a lot to put on a young fifteen-year-old. You know, at some point, you need to have a conversation with your parents about *who* you are. They deserve to know the truth about your sexuality. If they don't like it—then it's really their problem, not yours. Why don't we continue our conversation on Friday at the same time?"

Christopher nodded back in agreement. "Thanks, I appreciate your kindness. Honestly, I don't think I've felt this good in years." Smiling warmly, he stood up, shook Jason's hand, and left his office.

CHAPTER EIGHT
Susan Visits

Susan showed up on Thursday afternoon to visit with one of Christopher's favorite treats—a café mocha from Starbucks. "What a nice surprise, thanks so much." He took a big sip, savoring the sweet and bitter flavor before swallowing and put on a big smile.

Waiving a dismissive hand, she replied, "You're more than welcome. It's no trouble at all. Thought it might bring you a little bit of happiness."

"Just you being here gives me all the happiness I need. Still—I really appreciate the gesture." Taking another sip, "Mmmmm, this is so delicious. It's like you brought me a piece of salvation from the outside world."

"Well, go ahead and enjoy it. You look fantastic! In fact, I can't remember the last time I saw you looking this good. You seem to have a much better spirit than I've seen in—I can't remember how long. Tell me what's been happening."

"Gosh—where do I begin? I've been experiencing a lot of emotions—or rather releasing a lot of pent-up feelings." Before he could continue, they were interrupted by a knock on the door. "Come in please," he said raising his voice.

It was Jason, who entered the room. "Hi—Oh, I'm sorry, I didn't realize you had company. I can come back later."

"No, that's not necessary. I don't mind at all. Please, come in. I'd like to introduce you to my friend, Susan." Turning his head towards her, "This is the Mr. Calhoun I texted you about—the social worker."

Jason extended his hand out to shake hers and introduce himself. "Please, just call me Jason. It's a real pleasure to meet you. Christopher speaks so highly of you. You apparently have been an incredible friend to him."

"I'm very pleased to meet you. He's such a sweetheart; at least when he's sober," Susan said with a hint of sarcasm. *And you're just as beautiful as he said you were. Oh, look, no wedding band. He's single,* she thought to herself while projecting a big smile.

"Why yes, he does look very good I think," glancing over to his patient. "And I hope he *continues* to stay sober. I was just dropping by to check on you before I go home for the day. I wanted to see how you were feeling after our session yesterday."

"I feel *wonderful*. Thanks for asking. Trust me, I'm never going back to alcohol, I swear," Christopher said with conviction.

Jason gave a nod, "As much as I appreciate your enthusiasm, just remember, the outside world is not as protective as Watermeadow. You're kind of in a cocoon here. Once you leave—you're going to have to face the stresses of day-to-day life, which may set off your anxiety again. You must learn to survive those stresses without turning to alcohol. That's my ultimate goal for you. So, please keep that in mind. Although I must confess, I have lot of optimism for your success. I'll arrange to get you a prescription for Ativan or Xanax when you're discharged. That's a whole lot less destructive than using alcohol. However, the doctors are going to keep an eye on your use of that as well. I don't want you to stop abusing one drug just to get hooked on another. Still, you will need something."

"I get that. You're right, I will need to cope without alcohol. I have to believe in myself."

"Well, good. Very good. Then I'll see you tomorrow morning as scheduled. We still have some issues to tackle. Okay?"

"Yes, can't wait. I'll be there tomorrow," Christopher said with intensity.

"Oh, you can't wait now!" Jason chuckled. "Well, I do like the enthusiasm." Turning his attention back towards Susan, "Again, it was a real pleasure to meet you. You both have a great evening."

"It was a pleasure to meet you as well," she said. Jason left the room and softly closed the door as he exited.

"Damn!" she exclaimed. "He's as hot as you said he was!"

"Yeah, I know he is! But he's also so very genuine and kind-hearted. A really remarkable guy. He's helped me out so much."

"Oh, sweetie," Susan said with puppy dog eyes.

"Oh no, you have that look."

"What look?" she asked, trying to act innocent.

"You know what I mean; that look which says you're going to ask me to do something likely to embarrass the shit out of me," he retorted.

"Who? Me?" Susan asked with an angelic voice.

"Yes. You. Okay, let's have it. What do you want?"

"Ask him if he will go out with me?"

"What? Now you want me to play the role of a matchmaker?"

"Come on," Susan said in a whiny voice. "I haven't been out on a date in a long time. Hell, I haven't gotten laid either."

"Great! Now, I'm a pimp as well."

"Please—for me. Pretty please?"

"Okay, okay—I'll do it. It can't be any more embarrassing, or as painful as the other things I've shared with him already."

"Like what things," she asked with a concerned tone.

"You're my closest friend, so I might as well tell you some of the shit that has been eating away at me."

Over the period of fifteen minutes, Christopher then relayed to her the whole long yarn about his relationship with Richard and the unfortunate suicide it ended with.

"Yes, I remember him—and that terrible suicide. Oh, my God. You never told me any of this before! I'd no idea why he killed himself. And if he didn't leave a note, how would his parents ever know why he did it. Were you in love with him?"

Lamenting, "I think I was—or at least a huge crush. I was so devastated, and my father never wanted to revisit that whole episode. I knew at that point my dad would *never* accept me as being gay. I bottled up that fear so much, I never wanted anyone to know. Except you. You're the only one I've opened up to about my sexuality. Richard's parents sold their home and moved away. I can't remember where they went." After a pregnant pause, he went on, "They couldn't stand being in that house with their images of seeing him in that mess of blood. Almost as if Richard's ghost was haunting them. You know—the thing that was terribly heartbreaking was the fact he was an only child. No other children to console them. So, it just became too painful for them to live there."

Susan took his hand, "You know I'd love you no matter what. I'm so sorry you had to go through that. It must have been so hard on you." Susan's tone shifted into something more serious. "Now, you listen to me. You're a grown man. You're not a little boy any longer, nor are we in high school. To hell with your father, if he can't accept you for who you are. Listen—if you need a place to stay when you get out of here, you can stay with me. Just until you get back on your feet. After finding a new job."

"Really? Do you mean it? That could be really helpful. I don't think I'll be able to afford my place now."

"Of course, I mean it. Especially since you're going to get me a date with that gorgeous hunk of a man." She felt she needed to break the tension now present.

"That's fair," he smirked. He embraced Susan in a big hug. "Thank you. You're the best friend in the world!"

"You're darn right I am! I love you even if you *are* a little fucked up. And I always will."

CHAPTER NINE
The Confrontation

S uddenly, another knock at the door came without warning. "Come in, please," announced Christopher. Nate and Maggie Parker pushed the door open, "Oh, hey Mom and Dad."
"Hi, sweetheart," his mother said as she entered his room. "Susan! What a lovely surprise finding you here too. It's always so nice to see you." Susan gave his mother a hug.

Nate leaned in as well to give her a hug. "You look more beautiful each time I see you. You always brighten my day."

"Why thank you, that's so sweet of you to say," she said cheerfully. If there was one thing Christopher was spot-on about, it was the fact that his parents adored her! Couldn't have asked for a nicer girl if she had been their daughter.

"So true; you look more beautiful each time we see you," Maggie added, emphasizing her husband's point.

"You both are just too kind!" said Susan.

"We're just stating the obvious," said Nate.

"She's such a lovely girl." Maggie continued, "I don't know why you and Christopher never developed a romantic interest."

"I think Dad probably knows the real reason why," Christopher said while turning his attention to his mother.

"What are you talking about?" His mother asked.

Now, being austere, he said, "Why don't you tell her the truth, Dad? You know why the two of us never became romantic. Don't you?"

"Why on earth would I know why your relationship never blossomed?" His father asked.

Susan was becoming increasingly uncomfortable with this conversation, "Oh, honey, is this the time and place?"

Speaking up for himself at last, Christopher began, "I need to get this shit out in the open, once and for all. Earlier this week, my parents complained I wasn't willing to talk about what was bothering me, as to why I kept drowning myself in alcohol. I've shed more painful tears in the last few days than I can remember in my entire life." Turning his attention back to his father, "So, Dad, are you going to stand there and say you've *no idea* as to why the two of us, me and Susan, never became romantic? Have you forgotten about my friend, Richard Hoffman?"

Maggie exclaimed, "Oh my God! I remember the boy. Oh dear, such a tragedy. His parents never could understand why he shot himself. Nate, what is he talking about? What do you know? Why didn't their relationship ever become romantic? Is there something you know, and you're keeping it secret?" It became apparent Nate's wife was becoming annoyed.

"Why are you getting cross with me?" Nate asked in a curt tone.

"Because I've seen other situations during our marriage where you've hidden issues from me! What do you know about that poor boy? Do you know why he killed himself?" Maggie asked.

Susan and Christopher had taken a seat on the small couch. She was clutching his left upper arm. "I'm here for you, honey—all the way," she whispered to him.

"I know you are. Thanks," he whispered back, then continued. "Why can't you just tell Mom the truth? You can't say the words—can you? Tell Mom exactly what you saw Richard and me doing in my bedroom when you walked in on us? What did you see with your own two eyes? And you forbade me from ever telling Mom! You've been ashamed of me all these years, haven't you? I may not be perfect, but I'll be Goddamned if I'm going to continue to be ashamed of who I am? I am, what I am, Dad!"

Nate remained silent and gave no response. He collapsed down onto the reclining chair, falling into what appeared to be a hypnotic trance. The memories of that day and his son, then only fifteen-years old, came crashing over him like a tsunami. All those memories and emotions he'd buried in the depths of his mind. The guilt and deep remorse about what happened. The news coverage of the terrible, painful event. The images of the young boy found in a pool of blood, which had been published in all the local newspapers.

Although twelve years had now passed, he was forced to recall what he saw on that fateful day. Sighing in discontent, "I think—what he's trying to say is..." Nate paused, "that he's gay. Is that what you're trying to hint at?" He continued, "For I can believe that's the *one* thing that would be sure to kill any chance of your relationship evolving into something more."

Christopher's face took on a glazed expression, "Yes, Dad, that's exactly it. So, you've *known* the truth all these years, haven't you?"

Drawing in a deep breath and letting it out, Nate replied, "I suppose on some level, yes, I have. I didn't want to accept it. I'd rather not accept it now, but what choice are you leaving me?" Nate paused, "All I wanted to do was pretend that I never saw what I obviously saw. The shame and embarrassment I felt that day at the fear of having a gay son. The two of us were so close. And I got so angry," he said with a note of hostility. "Did you have feelings for that boy?"

"Yes, Dad, of course I did."

Nate said, "Now, looking back, it's so obvious."

Christopher teared up and exploded, "You completely destroyed my self-worth that day; I was crushed! Like—I was damaged goods!

Oh, I was a terrific son, and you loved me, just as long as I wasn't queer. And the one person on the planet who accepted me just as I was, killed himself. I felt entirely responsible for his suicide. If you hadn't caught us, and you hadn't exploded at us, he might still be alive." Trying to fight back the tears, "Look—I know now it wasn't my fault. Richard was the one responsible for pulling the trigger. But my heart still aches for what could have been."

A look of astonishment covered Maggie's face, and she rounded on her husband, "Heavens! Why on earth did you keep this to yourself? Who were you trying to protect? Me? I don't need your protection from the truth. Better yet, I don't want your protection from the truth either. Damn it, Nate, you *stupid* old man! I love you, but from now on, don't you *ever* hide anything from me again." She was so pissed.

Nate walked over to Christopher and took his hand, "Can you ever forgive me? I've been such a fool. Or a stupid old man as your mother puts it. I realize it now. You're not my little boy anymore; you're a grown man. I'm sure you know who you are by now, and I will trust everything you tell me. If I *have* to accept you being gay, so be it. I'm just going to have to get past my prejudice. I'm only sorry I didn't communicate it to you on that day when your friend… Oh God! What have I done?" Nate began to choke up, "Can you please—please forgive me?"

Christopher's anger and upset softened as he took in his father's plea. He stood up and put his arms around his father, "Yes, I'll forgive you," he sobbed. "I can't change who I am. Nor can I explain to you why I'm gay. It's just the way I'm wired."

Susan had tears flowing down her face, "Good grief! Now you all have me crying too."

Maggie asked Susan, "Did you know he is gay?"

"Yes, I did. I've loved your son for what seems like forever. I wanted our relationship to be *more than friends.* In case you two haven't noticed, your son is *incredibly handsome,* but he has always been honest with me. As much as I love him, I can't make him into something he isn't. Then what kind of friend would I be? He has such a good heart, even though he's made some incredibly unwise decisions. I just can't imagine my world without your son in it. But so, help me God!" letting her emotions get the better of her, "If your son gets himself mixed up with alcohol again, I'll personally bash him over the head!" Susan said in a softer voice, "I'll be done with him. I can't cope with it any longer. He knows this."

Maggie turned to her son, "I can't imagine my world without you in it either. And what the hell is wrong with you being gay? It's who you are, and I don't care what anyone says, it's what *God* expected you to be. I don't understand why it makes such a difference to people, other than just pure bigotry!" Taking in one deep breath to calm herself down and to break the heavy tension, "Yes, he's quite the looker. Somehow, the combination of our genes worked rather well in his favor." She asked Christopher, "So tell me, do you have a beau?"

Christopher looked at his mother with a confused expression, "What's a beau?"

Nate and Maggie laughed. Susan and Christopher just looked at each other bewildered, while he shrugged his shoulders, since they couldn't figure out why that question was so funny. Finally, his father said, "Oh, sweetheart, a *beau* is what your mother used to call me. It's a very old-fashioned word for a boyfriend. That's all. Not that I ever dreamed of asking my son this question, but I had better get used to it. So, do you have a beau?" Now he was trying to lighten the mood in the room.

Christopher just smiled, "No but I have Susan, thank God. I certainly would love a boyfriend. I don't want to be alone the rest of my life. But it'll have to wait until I have put my life back together."

"My life is perfectly together, and I would love a boyfriend," Susan interjected.

"Well, we'll do our best to keep our ears and eyes open for both of you," Maggie said. Now puzzled, "Although I must admit, trying to find a boyfriend for my son is a challenge I've no idea how to tackle." With that comment, all four broke out laughing.

CHAPTER TEN
Unexpected Visitor

Nate and Maggie Parker were home for the evening in their seven-thousand-square-foot home, located on the Southwest side of Indianapolis. Their home exuded opulence at every level. From the elaborate faux-painted walls or expensive wallpaper throughout, to high-end traditional furniture. The kitchen was done in a French country motif, and each bathroom had highly ornate vessel sinks accompanied by elaborate decorative hardware. Appointments like Lalique and Swarovski crystal figurines were used to heighten the interior design. The china hutch in the dining room displayed Royal Doulton dishes that cost two-hundred-fifty dollars a setting and were trimmed in fourteen-carat gold. No doubt they had excellent taste, but it often carried a high price tag.

Nate made his fortune as a very successful corporate attorney, a self-made multimillionaire who came from humble and modest roots. He took immense pride in his work and always gave one-hundred percent of himself when taking care of his clientele. Protecting his clients' interests and their reputations was undoubtedly his highest priority, even if his customers' business practices sometimes fell outside of what most would say was ethical or legal. If his clients fucked up, he'd take care of the cleanup, so to speak, at their expense. His clients maintained good reputations, and they wanted to keep it that way. He became famous for his talents, at making his customers' dirty laundry go away—permanently. Although, to be clear, he was never going to murder someone to avoid public embarrassment for the benefit of his clientele. Even he had his limits of what he was willing to do.

Still, he'd do almost anything in his power to keep his clients happy. Client confidentiality was always imperative in any lawyer-client relationship. But it was his talent and ability to tidy up their faux pas that drew in loyal followers, and now that was how he made most of his fortune.

They had just finished eating dinner when the doorbell rang. Nate called to Maggie, "I'll get it, honey." Upon opening the door, he found a gentleman, who was his most prestigious client; at least he considered him to be so. "Good evening, Sam," he greeted Mr. Barron with a smile. "What a pleasant surprise! What brings you here?"

"I wanted to drop off those documents you requested."

Nate extended his hand to take the file folder from him. "Oh yes, of course. Thank you so much. But you didn't have to bring the papers to my home. I'd have been happy to send a courier to fetch them. I want to make it convenient for you," he said with emphasis.

"That's very kind of you, but it's really no bother. Your house isn't all that far from mine, and I've been cooped up at home all day. I desperately wanted to get out for some fresh air and coming over here gave me that much-needed excuse."

"Okay, well, in that case, I'm glad I could accommodate you with a distraction. Nevertheless, it's always so good to see you. Please come in and sit down. Make yourself comfortable. Can I get you something to drink?"

"Thanks. Perhaps some of your wife's famous mint iced tea which I love so much. That's, if you have some."

"I believe she made some this morning, in fact. Hey, Maggie, Sam Barron is here. Please come and say hello," he said with a loud voice.

He went to the kitchen, leaving their guest sitting in the living room. She went to greet their guest with a hug. "Good to see you again," she said. "What brings you by tonight?"

"I was dropping off some papers to your husband. Plus, I was just telling him that I'd been in the house all day and was desperate to get out."

"It's a nice treat to have you visit us. How's your wife doing?"

"Patsy is doing just fine. Thanks for asking. Viatone has been keeping me quite busy myself. I'm becoming a little burned out."

"Perhaps you should take some time off," she suggested.

"Too busy; I can't afford to take the time off right now. Maybe in a few months."

Nate arrived back in the living room to hand Sam his iced tea.

"Thank you," he said. Nate then took a seat on the couch beside Maggie.

"How have you both been?" Sam asked. "It seems like I haven't seen you guys in ages. I mean, Nate and I talk on the phone all the time, but it's just not the same as being able to relax and have a conversation."

"We've been fine for the most part," Nate replied. "Suppose we're not perfect, but then who is?"

"No, I guess you're right. It's rare that any of us is, but perfection seems to be a concept we all strive for. Tell me, how are your boys doing, particularly, Christopher?"

Completely caught off guard and astonished, "Why—what do you know about him?" Maggie asked.

Sam suddenly realized they didn't know he knew about their son's rehab treatment. *But why and how would Sam Barron know?* Was the thought racing through Maggie's mind. This was a family issue which they hadn't broadcast to any of their friends and only told a few close relatives.

"Uh—um—well, you see, he told me he was going into Water-meadow for rehab," he said in a frightened stutter. "I ran into him—fairly regularly at Starbucks. I guess a favorite spot for each of us." That was true; Christopher had discussed his rehab with Sam.

"He did?" Nate asked. "Why, I had no idea that you and my son were that—uh, close."

"We're friendly I guess. Always has been a bright young man. I—uh—tried to visit him today, but security wouldn't let me in. I seem to have been placed on a blacklist of sorts. I think there must be a mistake somewhere down the line. I can't see why he wouldn't want a visit from me." Of course, he knew *goddamn* well why he'd been blacklisted! But he couldn't possibly let Christopher's parents know the reason why.

"You must forgive us. The fact you know where he is, has taken us by complete surprise. We're somewhat—shocked!"

"Yes, I—uh—can understand that. I was just concerned about his well-being—that's all. I honestly didn't mean to alarm you. And I certainly don't want to pry."

Maggie sighed, "Well, if he told you, I guess there isn't any reason for us to be concerned about your knowledge. He can certainly share the information about his circumstances with anyone he is comfortable with."

Nate nodded, "I suppose I have to agree with Maggie. Honestly, he's doing quite well. We spent time with him today, and although it was a bit of a confrontational visit, he looked good. Very good, in fact."

"That's great news to hear! By the way, Maggie, your iced tea is delicious as usual." Sam felt it might ease the tension in the conversation by giving Maggie a compliment.

"Thank you," she said.

He continued, "Although I'm sorry to hear that your visit turned confrontational. Nothing too serious I hope?"

"Goodness! Not certain how to respond to that...," Nate trailed off. "It was a rather serious conversation, and his feathers were *certainly ruffled*, but I think we both feel like most of his emotional issues were resolved. So, we feel good about how we left things today."

"It all sounds quite positive. I certainly wish your son very well. I am sorry I wasn't allowed in to visit him in person. But if he's doing well, I suppose that's what matters most."

"It's rather odd," she said. "I mean, why of all people would you be blocked from visiting him? I suppose we can ask and find out why."

"Uh—well—I mean—you guys don't have to make a fuss just for me. If he's safe and doing well, that's what's most important. I guess I should call it a night. Thank you, guys, so much for the company and the refreshment."

"It was good of you to stop by." Nate stood up to show their guest to the door. "Always happy to catch up with you. You take care now." Sam left, and Nate closed the door behind him.

"I have to say that was a most peculiar conversation! Why do I feel like something is going on between Sam and Christopher we're not supposed to know about?" Maggie asked.

"I was thinking the exact same thing. It's as if he simply used those documents as an excuse to drop by just to check on Christopher. It's very odd!"

"I agree, it's strange. Let's visit Christopher over the weekend and see what he has to say. But listen, Nate, if he isn't comfortable talking about it, *don't* push him. Our son has made great progress, and I want to keep it that way. What he told us today—it took a lot of guts. I want him to feel safe talking to us about anything. I'm afraid if we push too hard, the relationship we have now might regress."

"Okay—I understand. For right now, all I want to do is just relax, and watch some television."

"I'll join you in the family room in a moment, as soon as I finish putting the leftovers from dinner away."

CHAPTER ELEVEN
Another Therapy Session

Christopher arrived at Jason's office, conscientious about being on time. "Come on in and have a seat," Jason said.

"Thanks," Christopher said wearing a grin.

"So, tell me—what would you like to talk about today?"

Putting on a fake smile, Christopher said in a forced, cheerful tone, "Nothing in particular."

Based on the body language he was receiving from his patient, Jason wasn't buying it. Leaning back in his desk chair, "Now you're just avoiding on purpose something you're not comfortable discussing. We've come a long way. I was hoping you'd feel happy telling me anything by now. What more can I do to gain your trust?"

"Please don't be angry with me. I truly think the world of you."

"I'm not angry, but I'm somewhat disappointed."

Letting out a big, deep sigh. "Like I just said, I think the world of you! As far as I'm concerned, the sun rises and sets over you. I guess you're close to my age, and I feel like you're one of my best friends now, as opposed to a social worker who's trying to help me put my life back together. I know we only met earlier this week, but it feels like it's been a whole lot longer."

"And...?" Jason asked in a prolonged questioning voice.

"And I know what you're driving at. Who is Sam Barron, and what the heck is going on between the two of us?"

After hearing all of this, Jason began to sense, based on his patient's bashful demeanor, that he was developing a slight infatuation towards him. Now, he was no stranger to his patients developing such emotional attachments. It came with the territory. Although he was more accustomed to female patients developing a crush on him. Still, he never let it bother him, rather he would simply roll with it. Leaning forward and resting both elbows on his knees, "You're sweet, and you have a remarkably kind heart. I appreciate you being honest about your feelings towards me. You're correct though. I'm trying to help you put your life back together. You see, to a great extent, your success becomes my success. The well-being of my patients is extremely important to me. Trust me, if I have to advocate on behalf of a patient, there's no one with as much passion as me. In regard to Sam Barron, I *certainly* know who he is! No explanation needed on that."

"Yes—I'm sure you know who he is. How could you not; he's famous enough."

"Look, I'm not forcing you to talk about Sam Barron per se. You made it abundantly clear that you loathe the man with every fiber of your being. But is it Mr. Barron, or is there some other topic you're avoiding that's somehow connected to him?"

"Jason, I think you're the bomb! And since you seem so much more like a friend…" A pregnant pause slipped in. "I—I don't want you to think less of me because of what I need to tell you."

"After everything you've shared with me, trust me when I tell you, I won't think any less of you; I promise." Giving a slight tug on Christopher's shoulder to gain his undivided attention, "Please look at me." Christopher moved his gaze up towards Jason's face. "I swear to you, you have my word. You have nothing to be frightened of. Regardless of whatever your past behavior has been like, you're still a good, decent person. So, please, talk to me."

Letting out an apprehensive sigh, Christopher continued. "My college degree is in engineering."

"I see, a math wizard!" he complimented.

"Very much so. Anyhow, after I graduated from college, I had a good, respectable job at Jacobson Engineering. I did very well with it for the first couple years, and then my drinking started getting in the way."

"I take it that alcohol cost you your job."

"Not just my job, but my entire career! I couldn't get a decent job reference; people talk, you know. No one wanted to hire me."

"I see, that must have been a challenging time."

"Worse than that, I couldn't pay the rent on my fancy apartment. I needed money—and I was too ashamed to ask my parents for help."

"So, what did you do?"

With every ounce of courage Christopher could muster, he finally shared the most humiliating aspect of his past. "I became—an escort. Hell, I might as well be brutal, a prostitute!" He continued in a frenzied voice, "I was so desperate; I didn't know what to do. I didn't want to be evicted and left out on the streets. I just figured I could..."

Picking up where Christopher left off, Jason joined the dots. "You figured, that rather than starve to death and be homeless, you'd cash in on those awesome good looks of yours, to make money. Does that sound about right?"

"Well—yes. I'm so ashamed of myself. I'd fallen so low, and all over alcohol. Now you know why I was so concerned you'd think less of me. I respect the hell out of you. I look at you and think you're so put together, smart, and successful. I look at myself and see nothing but a total fuck-up."

"Look—I won't pretend that I've ever been in those circumstances. Events that made you feel so desperate, you felt as though prostitution was your only choice for survival. Still, I can empathize with you." Christopher's eyes began welling up with tears, which

Jason was quick to notice. He reached over and briskly rubbed the top of his head, "It's okay, It's okay. I told you already I won't think any less of you. Not now, not ever. You can't drive yourself crazy worrying about what others think of you." He reached below Christopher's face to cup his chin. Then tilting his chin upwards, causing him to look him, right in the eyes. "More importantly, I don't want you to think less of yourself. That's probably the core of the problem that's wreaking havoc with your emotions. You have so much pent-up shame."

"You're right—I do!"

Jason sighed, "Isn't it time?"

"Time for what?" Christopher asked with a face that clearly showed he was at a complete loss of understanding.

"Isn't it time that you let go of that shame? Isn't it time you stopped beating yourself up for every mistake you ever made in the past? Stop beating yourself up about every person you think you wronged. If you did wrong, then *be a man* and apologize. Stop beating yourself up for having *been* a prostitute. In the simplest of terms, stop beating yourself up for your past behavior and for every poor choice you think you've made. Because—despite your past errors, you're a *decent* human being with a super warm heart. Susan sees that. So, why can't you?"

"I guess I just have a lot of old, bad tapes replaying in my head," Christopher frowned.

"You sure as hell do! Now I want you to repeat after me. 'I've nothing to be ashamed of. I take ownership of all my past actions and acknowledge I did wrong. I'll do my very best to make better choices going forward. Under no circumstances will I ever resort to the use of alcohol as an emotional crutch.' Go on now, I want to hear you say it back to me."

Christopher smiled at Jason with tears running down his face. "Ummm—I can't remember all that."

Jason coached him through every line of positive affirmation he had just recited. He then typed those sentences into his desktop computer and printed them out for Christopher. "I want you to read these affirmations to yourself every day. Three times a day. I'm going to delete those old tapes from your head. Even if I have to beat it out of you, damn it! I know this sounds silly, but trust me, reaffirming these concepts so often will do you a world of good."

Christopher gave him a big smile, "I will, I promise. You sure know how to save people from their own stupidity."

"I'm more likely rescuing you from your own naivety. Stupidity is a bit harsh." Jason sighed, "So, what does any of this have to do with Sam Barron, if I might ask?"

Christopher just stared back at Jason with an exasperated look on his face. "Come on! You're really going to make me say it aloud?"

A puzzled look washed over Jason's face as he stared back at him. Suddenly, his face became a mixture of astonishment and horror, just like an Agatha Christie novel, when all the clues fall neatly into place to solve the murder mystery. "Oh, my God! You mean Sam Barron was—a customer of yours? He used your services as a prostitute?"

"Yes, and please you can't say anything to anyone. Men like him would hire my services in exchange for my complete discretion. I kept their dirty little secrets. Although, I somehow think he's worried I'm going to talk or rather reveal the truth that he's really gay. His marriage is a total sham! I shouldn't be telling you this. But how else can I be honest with you."

"This discussion is completely confidential and whatever you tell me will never leave the confines of this room," Jason said.

"Our relationship went beyond just him directly purchasing sexual favors. He took a real interest in me—romantically. The man was married, and like an idiot, I fell for him. He was rich, powerful, and gorgeous. Instead of him buying my sexual services, he paid the rent on my apartment, my utilities, plus an allowance. I was so in love with him, I wanted more than he could give me. He was a married man hiding his sexuality from the entire world. He had to continue to portray himself as heterosexual to the world."

Softly groaning, Jason took over. "Oh, God, that's deep. Obviously, it wasn't a healthy relationship. Meaning, you also had to stay hidden in a closet, which is never emotionally sound. Plus, you became so beholden to this man. The man was completely taking care of you financially. He held all the purse strings."

"Everything you just said is absolutely correct. It became a toxic relationship!"

"And you wanted out of the relationship, but he wasn't willing to give you up without a fight?"

"Yes—how did you know?" Christopher asked with a look of amazement.

"Because I spend my time counseling all kinds of individuals and couples, and doing this kind of work, you eventually start to see patterns emerging."

"I see—meaning I'm just another sad fool who has fallen into this same pattern."

"Don't be so hard on yourself. After all, you're human, and as a rule, we all make mistakes. Let's not go down this rabbit hole again. Okay?"

"Okay. My story gets worse, though."

"How could it *possibly* get worse?"

"Well, after I finally managed to end our relationship, I went back to prostitution on a regular basis, and unbeknownst to me, Sam hired a private detective to follow me and obtain photographic evidence."

Rubbing his forehead with his right hand, Jason groaned, "Oh, good lord, it got worse."

"He wanted me back all for himself. The man says he loves me, but he has a twisted way of showing it. He threatened to send the photos to my parents, the press, and have them broadcast over the internet.

I still hadn't told my parents I was gay. I sure didn't want them to find out that way. Plus, the public humiliation of having those photos leaked everywhere."

"So, what happened?"

"I told him that if he pushed me, I'd go public with who he was. I'd tell the world his marriage was a fraud."

Jason grumbled, "Oh, good lord! You've gotten yourself into a *Mexican standoff!*"

"Yep—that's exactly where I am, and I don't know how to get out of it. That man has been emotionally and mentally torturing me. That's why I became so angry when he showed up."

"Of course. Now it all makes sense! To begin with, you need to tell your parents the truth about your sexuality. That way he can't possibly out you."

Leaning forward with excitement, Christopher continued. "I did! Yesterday afternoon, right after you left, my parents stopped by to visit. I confronted my parents with the truth. I went through that whole story about Richard and me. My father remembered everything, and he apologized for the way he treated me. As for my mother, she was totally cool with me being gay."

"That's such wonderful news! Congratulations! Stand up and give me a hug!" They leaped to their feet, embraced tightly, and rocked from side to side. "I'm so happy for you. That's such terrific news! You must feel so much better to get that weight off your shoulders."

"It's certainly a huge weight finally lifted off!"

"I bet it is!" With that, the two men let go of each other. "Well, I think we can stop for the day. I'll see you back on Monday, same time. You've made excellent progress. Considerably better than most. I think next week you can probably be discharged home. At least, I'll recommend it to the others on the team responsible for your care."

"Oh wow, back to reality," Christopher responded with hesitation.

"Now, I have to admit, I don't typically recommend or feel most patients can go home so quickly. However, I can tell you're an intelligent man and you recognize the harm you've been doing to yourself. More specifically, you've demonstrated the ability to recognize the issue or issues that gave you the desire to abuse alcohol in the first place. You really are a remarkable young man. Besides, don't you feel like you're ready? You can't stay here forever."

"No, I suppose not." In reality, Christopher didn't want to separate from this bond with Jason he was experiencing. Jason gave him an inner peace and filled his heart with a warmth he'd never encountered before.

Suddenly, Jason's face became alarmed. "Oh wait, I just realized something important. You need to have some blood tests done to check for any sexually transmitted diseases. Considering your alcohol use and your former profession, your risk is very high, I'm afraid. Do you think you were careful to always use condoms?"

"Yes, for the most part. But who am I kidding? With my drinking? I might have made some stupid decisions. Oh, dear God! Now I need to worry if I have HIV!" Christopher replied in a frenzied voice.

"Hang on, just calm down. You don't know whether you've anything to worry about. But we do need to find out. I'll ask your nurse to order the blood work straight away. It's still early enough to have the lab draws done. The sooner we get the tests done, the sooner we'll have an answer."

"Of course, you're right. Let's get them done." Now, completely racked with fear, "You think I could get another hug?"

"I think I can spare one." Jason held his arms open, and Christopher collapsed into his embrace. He had discovered how incredibly warm and comforting it felt when Jason held onto him. Never in his life had anyone's arms made him feel so safe and protected. Like nothing nor anyone could ever hurt him. More than anything, he wished he could be a bar of chocolate and simply melt in place. This was an experience he never wanted to end. As they weren't lovers, the hug had to end within an appropriate amount of time.

Letting go of the embrace, Christopher turned to leave. "Wait a second, I almost forgot!"

"Forgot what?" Jason asked.

"My friend, Susan, the one you met yesterday?"

"Sure, I remember her. What about her?"

"She's very observant, and she noticed that you weren't wearing a wedding ring."

Forcing a frown, "Sadly—I'm still single at thirty years old. I'd love to be married. Haven't found the right person yet."

"That's good for her, then! She thinks you're drop dead gorgeous and was hoping you might consider going on a date with her. This is incredibly embarrassing for me to ask."

"That's so sweet of her. And incredibly flattering of her to ask you to do it."

"So, what should I tell her?"

Jason took a seat in his desk chair and sighed, "Really—I'm truly touched by the offer. I truly am."

"But…?" Christopher began sensing this wasn't going to end well.

"I make it a point not to bring my personal life into work, but given the circumstances, I suppose there's no harm. To be perfectly honest, I'm not looking for a wife. I'm—looking for a husband."

With that bombshell dropped, Christopher immediately collapsed onto the small couch letting out a gasp and in wide-eyed wonderment. "You—you—you mean—you're gay?"

"Surprise!" Jason blurted out in response, using an upbeat and playful tone.

"Susan is going to have a shit fit! It'll be my fault for making it rub off on you."

"Yes, well, it doesn't work like that, you know."

"Oh, I most definitely know! I just can't understand, you're so smart and kind, and..."

"And what?" Jason asked with a wrinkled brow.

"And you're fucking beautiful! Pardon my language."

"Thank you. You're very kind to say so."

"It's true though! How is it possible that somebody like you isn't beating the boys off with a stick? You're such a catch."

"I must say, if you're trying to stroke my ego, it's working! I can tell you it's not for the lack of trying to find Prince Charming. I have this old saying, and for the life of me, I can't even remember where I first heard it. But the saying is, 'There's a lid for every pot.' I continue to believe that and hopefully..."

"You'll find the lid to your pot," Christopher finished his sentence.

"That's what I'm hoping for. Hey, I have a cousin. George Goldman is his name. He's single. He's always asking me to be on the lookout for single women. Perhaps I can speak with him about Susan."

"Is he cute? I only ask because that's going to be the first thing Susan will want to know."

"*I* think he is," Jason said confidently.

"Why not? Can't hurt to ask." Christopher scribbled down Susan's cell number on a piece of paper for Jason. "Okay, well, I'll let you get back to work. Thanks."

"You're welcome, and I know it's hard, but try not to worry. I'll see you on Monday." Jason opened his office door to show Christopher out.

Shit! I'd do anything to date that man, he dreamt to himself.

CHAPTER TWELVE
Jeremy Visits

Clear, sunny weather greeted Saturday morning. The air temperature was what Christopher considered to be perfect. It wasn't hot or humid, nor was it cold or rainy. There was a nice, gentle breeze that felt pleasant blowing across all the exposed parts of his body. And being summer, well, that only meant it wasn't winter. Good God, how he hated winter. Worse than hate, he loathed winter. Despised the bitter cold, snow, and ice. In fact, he took pride in the fact he'd never been skiing in his life. He hated snow with such passion that he couldn't envision why anyone would deliberately want to go and frolic in it. So, when it was spring or summer, he was always going to be much more content.

Watermeadow had a beautiful outside courtyard area, where patients could wander around and take in the fresh air. His brother, Jeremy, who was four years younger, was visiting, and they were both outside enjoying the magnificent weather. The two brothers hadn't always been very close growing up, but Christopher was hoping to change all that.

"Why didn't you ever tell me you were gay? I would've understood," Jeremy said. "What made you think I wouldn't have accepted you? It breaks my heart that you didn't feel comfortable enough to share this with me."

"Gosh, please don't feel bad. I had a hard time accepting it myself, little brother. Still, thanks for your support; it means a great deal to me."

"Sure thing," Jeremy smiled and gave his brother a quick hug.

The two boys took a seat on a bench when they both noticed Susan approaching. "Hi there!" Christopher greeted. "It's great to see you as always."

"I didn't know you were out here. I couldn't find you inside, so one of the nurses told me you had come out here for a walk." She then gestured with her arms and hands as if to separate the boys, "Scoot over you two so I can sit in the middle." The brothers obliged, and she plopped down between them. Staring right at Christopher, "So, tell me!"

"Uh—tell you what?" he asked back with puzzlement.

"What did Mr. Calhoun say about me? You know—about me wanting to go out with him?"

Christopher grimaced, "Well… uhhh… geez…"

"You did ask for me?"

"Yes—Yes, I did."

"So… What happened? What did he say?"

Jeremy was confused, but wanted to remain polite, "May I ask what you both are talking about?"

"Oh, sure!" she responded with bounding enthusiasm. "Your brother's case manager here is gorgeous and single. I asked your brother to see if he'd go out with me."

"Oh, I see," he said and smiled knowingly at her.

She redirected her eyes back towards Christopher. "So, go on… What did he say?"

"Uhhh… Well… You see…" Christopher was clearly struggling.

"Uhhh—that's all you can say. Wait—Jason doesn't like me! Is that it? How can he not like me?"

"No—he likes you just fine," he said definitively.

"Good—so what's the problem? Because based on your body language," she motioned with her right hand sweeping around the length of his body, "something is wrong."

"You're not going to like my answer," Christopher cowered. His voice was racked with trepidation, "You see—it turns out that he's—gay."

Her facial expression froze, while her lower jaw dropped. "He's gay! Are you fucking kidding me? Has every decent man on the planet suddenly turned gay?"

Christopher transformed into a shrinking violet, cringing in place.

"I'm having a heterosexual emergency here!" Jeremy started to laugh aloud.

"This is so not funny!" exclaimed Susan.

Jeremy cleared his throat, "Sorry, I didn't mean to laugh at you. Honest, I didn't. I was just laughing at the craziness of the situation. And I promise you, the entire male species has *not* gone gay. At least not yet." He chuckled again.

"I do have some good news!" Christopher suddenly spoke up. "He has a cousin who's available. I even gave Jason your phone number to pass on and see if his cousin would be interested. And yes, I already checked to make sure he's cute."

Susan was frowning in disgust, "Have you met this cousin? I mean, how do you know he's cute?"

"No, of course I haven't met the guy. But Jason has said he is cute. I figure, since Jason is gay, I think we can trust his judgment."

She sighed, "Guess I can't argue with that logic. How do you know the cousin isn't gay?"

Christopher stared back at her as if to say, *you must be kidding me!* "Come on now, give me a little credit. I'm sorry to disappoint you." He paused and raised his brow, "You know, I have to tell you, for what it's worth, I was just as flabbergasted as you. I never realized that Jason is gay."

"Well, shit!" she exclaimed. "I guess *you* can have him then."

"I wish," he said with reluctance. "Just because he's gay doesn't mean he'll ever consider dating a patient. It's a professional taboo anyway. Not to mention, he's going to want a guy who has his shit together, not a fuck-up like me!"

"You're being kind of hard on yourself," Jeremy said breaking into the conversation. "Give yourself some time to get back on your feet. Would you *really* like to date this Jason guy?"

"You better believe I would! I have to say I'd give my left nut to date a man like him—but then again—he'd probably find me more attractive with both balls intact."

Christopher's brother burst out laughing, "I'm sure he would like you to have two balls instead of one. But hey look, if you wait a few months, he might not feel like he's dating a patient. This guy could be the incentive you need to get your shit together."

"You honestly think so?" asked Christopher.

Susan interrupted, "Sure, why not? I mean—I wouldn't tell Jason that's what you want. If you let on that you're interested in him romantically now, it may scare him off for good. You'll have to prove yourself to be completely stable for him first. And there's no guarantee he'll wait for you either, unfortunately; just a risk you'll need to take." Susan shifted her view back to Jeremy, "What do you think?"

"I have to agree with her on this. If you approach this guy months from now, you stand a chance that he's going to see you in a new light. That's if, in fact, you make yourself a real catch for him; standing on your own two feet, taking care of yourself, a respectable job. If you want this guy bad enough, you're going to have to stay sober when you leave rehab."

"Dear God! That man would make me the luckiest guy in the world. He's such a great guy. Close to my age, smart, successful, and he's so beautiful to look at. I'd *love* to get into his pants," Christopher said with amorous passion.

Jeremy laughing, stopped him from continuing, "Please—no need to go any further. I don't need all the gory details."

"To hell with that, *I* want all the gory details," Susan interrupted.

Jeremy continued, "Hell, unless he pulls his shit together and morphs himself into Prince Charming, he won't ever get into this guy's pants. From everything I've heard in this conversation, something tells me this Jason wants more than just great sex."

Christopher rebutted, "I want more than just great sex myself. I want a great guy I can build a life with, together. I want real intimacy, friendship, and passion." He let out an impassioned sigh, "I want to fall in love and get married."

"So, do I," Susan said.

"Come on, guys, let's get up and walk. I want to get some exercise, and it's such a beautiful day." Christopher said quietly to himself, *would he ever really want me? Could he ever?*

CHAPTER THIRTEEN
Nate and Maggie Visit

"Excuse me," Maggie asked, "We're trying to find Christopher Parker. He doesn't appear to be in his room." She seemed a bit baffled, "Do you have any idea where he could be?"

"I'm sorry. I'm afraid I don't know where he is. Did you check outside in the courtyard perhaps? It's a beautiful day. Maybe he stepped out for some fresh air," said Jason.

"You're right. It's quite lovely outside. Could you tell us the quickest way there?"

"Certainly," Jason said, extending an arm to show the way. "Just follow this hallway down, and you'll see the sign pointing to the courtyard exit. Are you his parents by any chance?"

"Yes, we are," Nate said with a smiling, friendly tone. "And you are?"

Jason extended his hand to shake theirs. "My name is Jason Calhoun. I'm your son's case manager and social worker. It's very nice to meet you both. I'm not often here at the weekend, but I was trying to catch up on some paperwork."

"Thank you. It's our pleasure to meet you too," Nate said. "Could you give us an update on how Christopher is doing in terms of his re-hab."

Jason shrugged his shoulders, "Outstanding! Your son is quite a remarkable, bright, young man. I think, even though he has been with us for such a short time, he should be ready for discharge sometime next week."

"That's wonderful! That's so good to hear. Although it does seem rather fast to me," Maggie said. "Are you sure he's ready to go back home?"

"Yes, it's faster than most, I agree with you there. However, he made the choice himself of coming to rehab. Often, patients are here for much longer. In my experience, when patients voluntarily make the commitment of going through this process as opposed to a court of law compelling an individual to rehab, it tends to lead to much greater success. Now, don't get me wrong, just volunteering yourself to a drug rehab program is no guarantee. However, patients who come here voluntarily really do tend to be more successful. With all that being said, your son has made tremendous progress here, and I feel he *is* ready to go back to the real world and will lead a sober life. It's his choice, ulti-mately. I can't make him stay dry. He *has* to want it; no question about that."

"Well, I must say, I'm relieved to know he's doing so well," Nate said. "On another note," he threw in a bit of a pause. "Do you, by chance, have any idea why Sam Barron was barred from seeing our son? At least, it's our understanding, that he's not permitted to visit Watermeadow."

"Yes, I was responsible for having him banned, but only while your son is here. He isn't blacklisted indefinitely."

Maggie was baffled again, "But why is he banned from visiting Christopher? Although to be honest, we only just found out those two seemed to have some kind of friendship. We don't understand the nature of their relationship. Can you shed some light on it for us?"

Jason said, in a kind and diplomatic tone, "You will appreciate the reason your son wanted Mr. Barron barred is something I can't disclose. At least, not without Christopher's permission. I'm sorry, but patient confidentiality is something taken very seriously here. I can only say this, I wouldn't have suggested I could prevent Mr. Barron from attempting to see him if his reaction to the man's arrival wasn't so explosive. It was done in the best interests of your son."

"But he's *our son!*" Nate said sharply. "Don't we have the right to know about our own child?"

"With all due respect, Mr. Parker, your child—isn't a child. He's an adult. As my patient, I'm required to keep anything he shares with me during our counseling sessions, completely confidential. Surely, you both must understand that?"

"Yes, we do understand the need for confidentiality," Maggie said, although with exasperation in her voice.

"Look—for what it's worth, I should tell you both, despite your son's poor judgment in relation to his alcohol abuse, you guys must have done something significantly right while raising him. You should both give yourselves some credit for that. Your son has to be the sweetest, smartest gentleman with the kindest heart I've ever had the privilege to counsel. Remarkably intelligent! There's just something special about him that I don't encounter very often. He understands and recognizes the various triggers from his past as well as in his current life, which caused him to drink in the first place. If he can truly recognize the rationales of why he used alcohol and demonstrates the strong desire to be sober, then he has what he needs to remain dry. However, again, he has to want this more than anything else. He's the only one who can make that choice. That said, I've very good feelings about his success going forward. And I don't say that lightly, I can assure you.

Now, as far as Mr. Barron is concerned, why not ask your son. But it's entirely up to him as to what he wants to discuss with you."

Nate said nervously, "We suspect he may not be comfortable sharing what's going on with Mr. Barron. He's been secretive and has hidden some of his feelings from us for a long time on certain issues. Like the fact he's gay."

"Listen, Mr. and Mrs. Parker, I do appreciate everything you're saying. And you're right of course, he may not be ready to share everything about his life. As I've said, your son is a grown man. He's entitled to privacy just like both of you have the right to privacy in your lives. I think sometimes parents forget that."

"That's true. I suppose I still think of our son as our little boy on some level," Nate said with a choked-up voice.

Jason waved a dismissive hand, "Nothing wrong with that; most parents feel protective about their sons and daughters, no matter how old they are. Anyhow, take a look outside in the courtyard. Good chance you will spot him there, I bet. You both enjoy your visit. Good day." Jason gave them a wink and went back down the hall in the opposite direction to the courtyard, to his office to tackle his workload.

Maggie and Nate proceeded to the courtyard. Sure enough, Christopher was outside and apparently being entertained by Jeremy and Susan. Christopher spotted them heading his way. "Hi, Mom and Dad."

"We couldn't find you in your room, and a Jason Calhoun told us we might find you out here," Maggie said.

"Yes, he's my case manager here. Great guy! He's been helping me to get my head on straight, so to speak."

"He seems to be very impressed by your progress here, and he says he's got good feelings about you leaving Watermeadow. Do you know what you're going to do for work and paying the rent on your apartment after you leave here?" Maggie asked.

"Susan said I could stay with her until I can find work and get back on my feet."

"Oh, Susan, you're such an amazing friend! It's no wonder he thinks the world of you, and it's very kind of you to offer." Nate emphasized. "But son, you should know you're welcome to move back in with us."

Susan interceded, "It's not a problem for me at all. I want to do this for him. Really—I don't mind."

Christopher said gently, "Dad, I'm sorry, but I just can't move back home with you, please, try to understand."

"I guess I might have felt the same way at your age about moving back to my parents," Nate said trying to be tactful. "But I've a better idea. How about your mother and I pay your apartment rent, let's say for the next six months? And some spending money, to help you get back on your feet. With the contingency that you stay away from alcohol, of course."

Jeremy intruded, "That's a hell of a deal! I wouldn't pass up an offer like that."

"Do you mean it, Dad? Would you guys do that for me? Are you sure?"

Nate embraced his son tightly, "I mean every word. And you won't have to pay back a dime. I take full responsibility for your self-esteem issues, so perhaps this will make up for some of the damage," he frowned slightly with remorse in his voice.

"I can't thank you enough!" Christopher beamed with excitement.

"We only want you to be happy and self-sufficient. I do realize the importance of living openly and honestly." Nate went on, "Although I won't pretend it doesn't scare the hell out of me how others may treat you, being a gay man. The world is full of bigots! Considering my past behavior, I ought to know."

"It frightens me too, but I'm sick of being a closet case. That closet was suffocating me!"

"I'm sure it did. What about work?" Maggie asked with concern.

"Of course, I'd like to go back to engineering, but I think I've burnt my bridges because of my drinking."

"Perhaps I can poke around among some of my engineering clients for any upcoming job opportunities. At least convince them to give you an interview," Nate said with a hopeful voice.

"Thanks, Dad, I sure would appreciate any leads."

"Listen, Christopher, your mother and I would like to discuss something with you, in private."

"Uh, oh, I don't like the sound of that," Christopher answered nervously.

"That's okay, Susan and I can take off and give you guys some privacy," Jeremy said. "Hey, Susan—perhaps you'd like to join me for an early dinner, if you've no other plans."

"You know, that sounds like a fabulous idea! On a Saturday night, I'd enjoy the company. You can even pick the restaurant," Susan responded.

"Great! Let's get going then." Jeremy held out his arm, Susan took hold of it, and off they went.

Christopher waved to them, "Bye guys! Have fun." Turning his attention back to his parents, "Okay, folks, what's on your mind?"

Nate ran his fingers through his hair, "Your mother and I had a visit the other day from my client, Sam Barron." Christopher immediately snorted with displeasure. "It came to us as a surprise that you two have some sort of friendship."

Raising his eyebrows, "What exactly did he say?"

"Quite honestly, it all felt very peculiar to us. He explained to us that he tried to visit you, but apparently, you had him banned. Your mother and I didn't know what to think. As far as we knew, he wouldn't have known you were here. So, it took us by surprise when he brought up the topic of his concern for your well-being. Will you enlighten us? What's the nature of your relationship with him?"

"And that's it? He didn't mention anything else?"

Maggie said, "That was pretty much it. I recall him saying he'd occasionally bump into you at Starbucks. Like your father said, the conversation came across feeling quite peculiar. Mr. Barron came by to drop off some documents to your father, but it felt like that was just a pretense."

While rubbing the back of his neck and letting out a big sigh, Christopher replied, "Look, all I'm comfortable is simply saying to you that I hate the son-of-a-bitch! I don't want to see him or be anywhere around him. I can't go into more details than that right now—I just can't. Please don't pressure me. Please, I'm begging you both, just leave it alone."

Nate, now concerned, "Honey, your Mom and I love you. If Sam Barron is threatening you and putting you in any kind of danger, we want to help."

"I'll be all right, Dad. I promise you. I'm sorry if I seem to be behaving rather elusive, but you are going to have to give me some space and trust me on this. If you want to do anything, just tell him to keep his distance. I don't want anything to do with the man!"

Nate shook his head from side to side, "Okay, sweetheart. We won't badger you, and next time I see Mr. Barron, I'll tell him as kindly as possible to leave you alone."

He groused, "You don't have to be kind to that mother-fucker!"

"Christopher Kennedy Parker!" Maggie shouted. When she addressed her children by their full legal name, they knew their mother meant business. "Is that language necessary?"

"It is where he's concerned!" Christopher was letting his anger get the best of him. "All I want is for Sam Barron to stay the hell away from me. I don't want him to call me or try to see me. I don't want any part of him!"

"I got it, son!" Nate said. "But he's still one of my top clients. It's not like I can come at the man with a knife, which sounds like something you'd like to do."

"You bet I would! I'd love to cut the man's throat!"

"Okay, already! You've made your point. I just wish you could confide in us what's been going on. But okay—we won't push you, and you have our trust. Mr. Calhoun did tell us we should allow you your privacy when you needed it. So, your Mom and I will respect your boundaries. We just hope you will let us in sometime soon."

Christopher teared up a little, "Thank you both so much." He threw his arms around his father and mother simultaneously. Nate, feeling his precious son's embrace, hugged back tightly. Now that his son was sober, he felt like the old Christopher was coming back. And for now, their son was greatly relieved not to have to share the whole tawdry nature of his relationship with Sam Barron. Maggie took a step back and looked at her husband and son. She shook her head in confusion but smiled nonetheless.

CHAPTER FOURTEEN
Susan Receives a Surprise

Susan, having had a wonderful time with Jeremy the previous night, slept in late on Sunday morning. Although she would always sleep late on Sunday mornings whenever she could. In her mind, that's what Sundays were for. At least she would take advantage when she didn't have one of her soirées to take charge of.

The day was greeted by more beautiful, bright, sunny weather. So, she kept her blinds drawn shut to keep her room dark. She lived in a two-bedroom apartment, using one bedroom as her home office. It was on the northeast side of Indianapolis and was just a ten-minute drive to Christopher's place. She was always glad she was such a short drive from him when wanting to seek his companionship; at least until his use of alcohol became so out of control.

She had dined with Jeremy at one of his favorite Italian restaurants. After all, she'd promised he could pick out the place. He ordered the spaghetti and meatballs, straightforward and unpretentious, but mostly, he just enjoyed comfort food. She, on the other hand, ordered veal parmigiana; her palette was decidedly more extravagant.

Susan yawned and stretched out in bed, then gazed at the clock on the nightstand. The time of 11:15 was staring back at her. *Oh Lord, I ought to have gotten up by now.* Despite the comfort of her bed, she reluctantly dragged herself to the shower. After an invigorating scrub, she jumped out of the shower, quickly dried herself, and dressed in Sunday casuals. She greeted the day with a breakfast of toasted sesame seed bagel with cream cheese and a glass of orange juice; this was her idea of easy comfort foods.

While she was enjoying her bagel, her cell phone rang. She answered and heard an unfamiliar voice. "Hello," she greeted.

"Hi there, my name is George Goldman, and I'm trying to locate Susan Rogers."

"This is Susan Rogers, but I'm afraid you have me at a disadvantage. I've no idea who you are. How did you get my number?"

"Yes, of course, I got your number from my cousin, Jason Calhoun. I believe you met him at Watermeadow. He's a social worker there."

"Oh, heavens! Yes, you're the single cousin of his! My friend, Christopher, mentioned you."

"That would be me," George said rather sheepishly. "I must confess, I'm horribly nervous. I'm not used to calling a girl out of the blue to ask her out on a date. I've been trying to push myself out of my comfort zone."

"I didn't even know your name. All I heard was that Jason had a cousin who was open to being fixed up. That's why your name didn't ring any bells initially."

"I can understand that," George said in a warm, kind voice. He was trying to be conscious of coming across in the best possible light.

"Jason has been caring for my friend, Christopher, who's a patient there. Not sure if you heard, but I embarrassed myself by asking Christopher to ask Jason if he'd go out with me."

"What's so embarrassing about that?"

"Well, for one, I didn't know he was gay. After I learned that fact, I felt stupid and embarrassed. Come to think of it, I wasn't embarrassed right away. I was more stunned than anything; the embarrassment came later."

"Oh, that. You've nothing to be embarrassed about. It happens to him quite often; women wanting to go out with him. People always assume he's straight. As far as he's concerned, that's what's wrong in the world. People want to believe that everyone around them is straight."

"I've always thought that. I mean, I assume the majority of individuals are straight."

"And you'd be correct. Jason would just like to not have everyone feel that's the case."

"I guess I can see his point of view," Susan agreed.

"I do too. Anyhow, I asked him a while back to please pass his rejects on to me," George said in a nonchalant manner as if he was talking to one of the guys. He cringed immediately. "Oh my God! I can't believe I just said that. How awful that must have sounded. I didn't mean to imply you were a reject. I'm so sorry!"

Susan giggled, "It's fine. I understand exactly what you meant. So, I'm going to have to ask you as it seems like I'm always falling for gay men, are you *absolutely certain* you're not gay? *Please* tell me you're not gay."

George laughed loudly, "I promise you, I'm one-hundred percent heterosexual. You've nothing to worry about there. I like girls; that's definitely not a problem for me."

"Sorry, I just had to ask," she playfully said.

"No, your trepidation makes sense to me. That whole 'Once burned, twice shy' sort of thing."

She smiled, "Yeah, that's it exactly. You sound very nice, George. What did he tell you about me?"

"He said, you were an incredible friend to his patient. Also, that you came across as intelligent, and he said you were very attractive."

"Awwwww, that's sweet of him to say."

"He's an awesome guy. We've been very close all our lives. I hate to think of my life without Jason. So, any chance you might be free for coffee this afternoon? I always feel having coffee for a first date is less pressure than a formal dinner."

"I'd love to. What time and where?"

"Starbucks on East Oaklawn Boulevard at 2:30. Do you know where that is?"

"I sure do. Meet you there at 2:30. But, how will I recognize you?"

"Ummm— I'll be wearing a red shirt, so you can spot me."

"Sounds great, I'll see you soon then. Goodbye, George."

"Goodbye," he said in kind.

Susan shot a quick text off to Christopher.

Susan: Hey you, that cousin of Jason's just called me. His name is George.

Christopher: Good to hear it. So how did he sound?

Susan: He sounds super nice. We're meeting for coffee this afternoon.

Christopher: You didn't waste any time.

Susan: Guess not. I'll let you know how it goes.

Christopher: Okay, looking forward to details. I'll let you get ready. Bye.

Susan: Bye, sweetheart.

Susan showed up at Starbucks right on time. She hadn't told him what she would be wearing. *That was stupid of me,* she thought.

However, as soon as she walked into the coffee shop, she saw a gentleman sitting off to one corner wearing a bright-red dress shirt and with two large cups of coffee in hand.

"You must be George," she greeted him. Immediately, as if by pure instinct, she rapidly took in every feature and detail of his face and body as he stood to shake her hand. *Striking muscular build, clean shaven, dark ash-blond hair, looks to be a twenty something, light blue eyes, and wearing a smile.*

"And you must be Susan."

"That would be me. At the risk of embarrassment, I have to say, you're cute. I can see Jason didn't lie about that."

George blushed rapidly, "Thanks. I appreciate the compliment." He nervously combed his fingers through his hair, "I have to confess, I've never thought I was all that much to look at. Jason has been beating me over the head that I'm crazy. In fact, he keeps telling me that red is my color, which is why I wore this shirt," he said while sporting a goofy grin. "I also have to say he didn't lie about you either. You're simply beautiful."

"Thank you. That's very sweet of you to say."

"You're quite welcome."

"He's right; you look good in red."

He blushed again, "Oh, here, I bought you a coffee already, but I didn't know how you take it."

"Cream and sugar," she politely said.

He offered to add them for her, which she accepted, and he grabbed her cup and went off on assignment. He soon came back and sat down again. They continued their conversation, exchanging the basics of occupations, hobbies, interests, likes, and dislikes. Susan was so enchanted by him, she was hanging on his every word. It wasn't just his good looks. George demonstrated good manners, warmth, and a terrific sense of humor. He had a willingness to try new things and travel to unfamiliar places, which were appealing attributes as far as she was concerned. The two of them gushed for two and a half hours. Susan finally noticed the time was 5:00 already. "Heavens! I can't believe how long we've been talking. I'm truly enjoying myself though."

"I agree, this has been fun. Hey, would you like to go to dinner? No reason the conversation has to end."

"That sounds like a magnificent idea." Susan wasn't ready to stop the date yet either. "Where do you want to go?"

"Hmmm, do you have a cuisine preference?"

"I had Italian food last night. Perhaps Mexican?"

"I love Mexican food. I know an excellent place not too far from here. Would you like me to drive? I can bring you back here later to collect your car."

"Fine with me," she answered eagerly and off they went to what she felt promised to be an enjoyable evening.

CHAPTER FIFTEEN
Good News

C hristopher landed at Jason's office on Monday morning for his usual appointment. "Good morning."

"Good morning. I trust your parents found you on Saturday?"

"Oh yeah, my parents mentioned they met you. You suggested they look in the courtyard when they couldn't find me. Yes, they found me all right." Christopher was seemingly apprehensive.

"Let me guess; they brought up the Sam Barron thing?"

"Yep! I'm still not comfortable telling them about my past occupation."

"I said they could ask you about your relationship with him, but it was up to you what you wanted to share. They were hoping to get the information from me."

"But you kept my confidence?"

"Of course, you know I always would."

"I feel sort of bad about betraying Sam Barron's trust. Even if he *is* a total son-of-a-bitch."

"True, but sometimes, we don't have choices about telling the truth, or rather divulging issues we don't wish to. There are times that a higher calling has to let hidden truths come out. For example, let's say a teenage girl is hiding the fact that she is having sex with her boyfriend because she knows her parents won't approve. She discovers she's pregnant. Now, how is she going to continue to hide her behavior?"

"Yeah—I see what you're saying. I'm hoping that nothing is going to force that to happen. Rather, I won't be forced into telling my mom and dad *everything* about my past."

"I don't see any reason why you should." Jason noticed that Christopher still seemed preoccupied. "Is there something else on your mind? You seem a little off."

"Frankly, I'm scared of those blood test results."

"Is that what has got you so apprehensive?" he asked with great relief. "Your results were back early this morning. All the tests were negative. You don't have anything to worry about. No HIV or STDs."

"Oh, my God! Really? I'm totally clean?"

"Yes, you are. I can have a nurse give you a copy of the results. So, for God's sake, stop worrying."

Christopher felt a lump in his throat. He was ecstatic and especially grateful his poor choices of the past were leaving no permanent scars on his health. Tears of happiness trailed down his face.

Jason continued, "Listen, I'm sorry if I frightened you about the possibility of HIV. But it seemed too risky for you not to be screened for it."

"I'm so relieved! That's why I'm crying. Could I get one of your famous hugs again?"

Jason stood up with extended arms and teased, "I may have to start charging extra for these hugs." Christopher collapsed into his embrace. Incredibly relieved, sheltered once again in Jason's strong arms. For the first time since his admission to rehab, Christopher's heart felt so full of hope and possibility; like he could face the real world again. The bad memories and shame of the past could finally be put to rest.

"I would like to discharge you home on Wednesday. Is that okay with you?"

Letting go of the embrace, Christopher nodded his head in agreement. "I'll ask Susan to come pick me up. Oh, by the way, she and George went out already."

"Yes, I know about that too. George gushed to me late last night with how much he liked her. Perhaps, just perhaps, he'll be the last frog she will ever have to kiss. If there is one thing I've learned in life, it's that you need to kiss *a lot* of frogs just to find the one which will morph into a Prince."

"I get it. You're referring to that old fairytale. Right?"

"That's right. After all, we all deserve to have a Prince Charming…" Jason seemed somewhat pensive and distant now.

"Hey, is everything all right?" he asked with concern.

Jason snapped back to the present and reality. "I'm fine. Sorry, I didn't mean to drift off. You better let your family know you'll be coming home then."

"Will you be around tomorrow? I'd like to say a proper goodbye."

"You're not getting rid of me just yet. I still need to see you tomorrow."

"Oh—sure—what time?"

"It'll have to be at 9:00 in the morning."

"Okay, well then, I'll see you tomorrow morning. I can't thank you enough. You've been an absolute godsend."

"Thanks, it's nice to be complimented. More times than not I feel as if I'm never appreciated," he groused. "Enjoy the rest of your day. See you in the morning."

Christopher ran back to his room and made a call to Susan to ask if she could collect him on Wednesday afternoon. She agreed and assured him it was no difficulty. "I understand George was quite smitten with you."

"Did Jason tell you that?"

"He sure did! Just a few minutes ago."

"George was super sweet and really cute! I'm just as smitten with him."

"That's wonderful! It truly is. If anybody deserves some happiness, it's you."

"Amen! I couldn't agree more. Look, sweetheart, I have to go. I love you, and I'll see you on Wednesday."

"Great, see you then."

Christopher then proceeded to let his parents know about his discharge. Nate and Maggie Parker were just as delighted to hear their precious son would be returning home later in the week. "By the way," his father said. "I did speak with Sam Barron and asked him to respect your space and to keep his distance. Of course, he wouldn't tell me any more about your relationship than you. I don't understand why you two are being so secretive."

"I'm trying to keep it that way, Dad."

"No doubt," his father concurred.

"So, what was his response?"

"He promised me he would. Frankly, son, I really don't know how much I trust him, though."

"I appreciate your efforts nonetheless. I love you, Dad."

"I love you too, sweetheart. Goodbye."

After he finished making his phone calls, Christopher decided to go outside for some fresh air and exercise. There was one thing he knew, Wednesday would be here soon enough.

CHAPTER SIXTEEN
Therapy Ends

"I thought you might like some coffee," said Christopher while extending Jason a fresh, hot cup. "I wasn't really sure how you took it. So, I can soon run back to the kitchen to get whatever you need?"

Jason smiled back, accepting the coffee, "Aren't you the perfect gentleman this morning." He nodded, "Go ahead and have a seat; you don't need to run back. I keep a supply of my favorite creamer here in my office. And, thank you, it was very thoughtful. I do enjoy my morning coffee." *Oh boy! He's really starting to crush on me now.* Jason grabbed his creamer from the small refrigerator in his office while sensing the necessity to bring the conversation around to a topic more on point. "Before you leave Watermeadow, I wanted to discuss your future and planning for it. I know before you arrived here, your life had become—a bit of a mess. So, I want you to have a game plan going forward. The goal is to not wind up back here again. No more alcohol abuse—period. Sadly, patients often lapse back into substance abuse patterns because they never really take a hard look at what it's going to take to get back on their feet. I understand the stresses of life. And I know you realize you're not going to find the answers at the bottom of a bottle. Are you?"

Shaking his head to emphasize his negative response, Christopher responded, "No, I'm not!"

"Where're you going to live? How are you going to support yourself? How will you handle any anxiety or panic going forward? These are key questions you need to ask yourself. Keeping these questions in mind, tell me about how you're going to tackle these concerns."

"Well—um—to begin with, my parents offered to pay the rent on my apartment for the next six months. Remaining sober was a contingency of course, as well as it should be."

"You're a blessed man! Take advantage of your parents' generosity but *don't* squander it. Many don't have the advantages of parents like yours. I'm fairly confident they are giving you a six-month deadline to put some pressure or a 'sense of urgency' on you to act on finding a job. Based on the conversations you and I had, I assume you don't wish to go back to your most recent occupation."

"No! Not only no, but hell no! I'm through with degrading myself. It would crush any ounce of self-worth I have left. Not to mention the risks to my health it puts me in. I've already had the shit scared out of me as a result of my drunken stupidity." Getting a little tearful, he continued, "I want to meet a great guy I can share my life with. Someone who treats and respects me for the good person I am. I'm worth it damn it! I know I am!"

Jason grinned and felt exuberant, *he gets it! Thank God almighty, he actually gets it. Something stuck!* "Yes—of course you're worth it. Obviously, your priority has got to be finding a job. Focus on taking proper care of yourself. All too often, alcoholics have a tendency to drink their meals and become terribly malnourished. Make certain you eat proper food. As your day to day life becomes stable, I'd encourage you to start dating again. Having a love interest will help keep you grounded."

"I'm worried about a potential boyfriend rejecting me because I used to be a prostitute."

Bobbing his head slightly, "I can understand being afraid of that. I can't promise you some men won't have an objection to it. And there's also no point in lying about your past. We all have a past, Christopher. It doesn't do us any good to try and run from it either. Hold your head up high and take pride in your recovery. It's a huge accomplishment! I promise you, the right man will see it. If he doesn't, then he wasn't meant for you. So, what do you wish to do for an occupation?"

"I want to go back into engineering. It's what I want more than anything else."

"That's very admirable."

"My dad is going to try to find me some leads on job opportunities. I'm horrendously worried about my past hurting my chances. I'm praying someone will give me a chance to prove myself. I know I have the abilities. I'm still smart enough."

"No doubt you are. You had a lot of animosity towards your father not very long ago. It sounds like he really cares about you. What's changed?" *Your dad is a hell of lot better than the jackass of a father I had!* The thought quickly flashed through Jason's mind.

"He apologized for his past mistakes, and he's getting used to the reality of having a gay son. He's learning to accept me as I am. Even if it means I love dick." Christopher winced, "Sorry, that was in extremely poor taste. Forgive me for my bad manners."

Letting out a small laugh and shaking his head, "It's okay. You're forgiven. My biggest concern for you is how you handle any stress and anxiety going forward."

"Jason, I swear to you, I'm not going to touch alcohol. Hey look, it's what got me into all this trouble in the first place. Cost me my career, my dignity, it cost me everything. If I'm having a meltdown, you said I could use an anxiety pill."

"Yes, that's perfectly fine, but only use them when you really, really need to. If anxiety starts to affect you on a more consistent basis, then by all means, ask your physician to start you on an antidepressant.

They'll give you more of an ongoing relief. There's no shame in admitting you need help. Do you have any concerns weighing on your mind right now?"

"Not that I can think of. Honestly, I'll be fine."

Jason wanted every patient of his to be successful after discharge. Although his concern for Christopher went beyond most other patients. In his mind, he was young still, and his potential for a good life somehow seemed more imperative. He saw so many repeat admissions from the patients he managed. *Please God, let him succeed*, passed through his mind. He sighed, "Good enough then, I'll let you go now, and I wish you the very best of luck."

"You're still going to be here tomorrow so I can say goodbye, aren't you?"

"Are you kidding me? I practically live here," Jason said with a subtle tone of sarcasm. "Fear not—you'll find me. Are your parents picking you up tomorrow?"

"Susan is coming to get me in the afternoon."

"Ah, Susan— even better."

"What's better?"

"Oh—never you mind for now. Enjoy the rest of your day. See you tomorrow."

CHAPTER SEVENTEEN
Final Goodbye

Wednesday late morning arrived, with Nurse Judy putting together all of Christopher's necessary discharge paperwork. She carefully covered all the essential details with him. He was educated on all the post-rehabilitation support groups Watermeadow had to offer and strongly encouraged him to attend. He assured her he'd participate as much as possible.

"Have you seen Jason this morning? I didn't catch him in his office earlier, and I wanted to say goodbye to him. I don't know how I can thank him enough, he's done so much for me."

"I haven't seen him this morning either, but I'll do my best to find him and see when he'll be here. Good luck to you. Jason and I are pulling for you."

"Thank you. I appreciate everything you have done for me."

Judy gave Christopher a nod and a smile, "You're so very welcome! Take good care of yourself."

It was 3:30 in the afternoon when Susan arrived to take Christopher back home to his apartment. "I'm still waiting to say goodbye to

Jason. I haven't seen him all day. My nurse told me she was going to try and find him, but I haven't heard anything yet. He said he was going to be here today, and I can't just leave without saying goodbye. At the very least, he deserves my gratitude."

She reassured him with gesturing hands, "It's fine. I'm not in a rush; we can wait a while longer."

"Thanks," he smiled.

Susan smiled back, "You're welcome. I can't get over how terrific you look. Wow! What an improvement."

Just then, the door to the room cracked open, and Jason peered in. "Hey guys, can I come in?"

Christopher sighed with great relief, "Are you kidding? I've been looking for you all day!"

"Judy told me you were looking for me. Sorry, I got caught up in some continuing education classes this morning. I promise you, I didn't forget my star patient is leaving. Good to see you again, Susan. Best of luck with George. Now, tell me, isn't my cousin the nicest guy?"

"He's the most wonderful man I've ever gone out with." Susan was radiant. "George is quite fond of you too."

"I'm just as fond of him. We've been close since childhood. Our mothers are sisters. He's a real catch, so don't let him slip away."

"I don't intend to," she reassured him.

Jason turned his attention back to Christopher and opened his arms for a hug. Wasting no time, Christopher grabbed his hero and clenched as tight as he could. Emotionally tearing him up inside was the thought, *will I ever see you again?* Christopher never wanted to let go of him. Jason rubbed Christopher's back, attempting to heighten the warmth of the goodbye.

At last, the hug subsided. Jason held Christopher's face between his two palms. "Okay, so, listen up my green-eyed beauty. You go out into that world, and you make me proud. Please stay strong. I know you can do it. But *you* must know you can do it. And you must want this sobriety more than anything else. Nothing is more important. Your mental, emotional, and physical health all depend on it."

Jason let go of his face. "Susan, will you be a dear. I need you to do me a huge favor. When you get back to Christopher's apartment, please go through it with a fine-tooth comb and toss every bottle of alcohol you can find down the sink. Don't leave any spot without searching. Every drawer, every closet, every nook and cranny in every room." Looking directly towards Christopher, "I expect you to help her with that purge. You're not to ever bring any alcohol into your home, not even for guests. Your *true* friends will understand. Remember, we talked about true friends?"

"I remember that talk, and I promise, I'll help her search and dump it all," he said. "Oh, that's the reason! Now I get it, that's why you were glad Susan was coming to fetch me."

Giving him a secretive wink, "If you need me, I mean *really* need me, you can call into Watermeadow and ask for me."

Nurse Judy had wandered by and was outside the door for much of this touching goodbye. Christopher grabbed his bags, and he and Susan departed Watermeadow to begin his life again. Clean and sober.

"Bye, Judy," he smiled at her as they walked away.

"Bye bye, sweetie." Judy turned and looked at Jason, "You know that boy has a major crush on you, don't you?"

He rolled his eyes, "So, it's obvious to you too."

"Darn right, it's obvious. However, what may not be obvious to you is that I think, perhaps you have a bit of a crush on him too," she smirked. "I know a crush when I see one."

Jason retorted with crossed arms across his chest, "Now, come on, you of all people should know that I would never date a patient."

"I know you wouldn't. However, considering that man just left our facility, it seems to me that he's not a patient of yours any longer. *He* might be the frog you've been hunting for."

"Even so, I need to know the guy has his shit together. You and I don't know if it's going to happen. Of course, it's what we hope happens."

"No, you're right. But you see what I see. And what I see is one of those rare patients who'll leave here sober and actually stay sober. It's true, I *don't* make that claim often, but it's what my gut tells me. He's going to do well. You and I have worked together for a long time now. In your experience, isn't that what your gut is telling you?"

Jason didn't respond, but wrinkled his forehead and bit his lip. He just stared out of the window noticing Christopher and Susan walking towards the parking lot. A pensive expression washed over his face.

CHAPTER EIGHTEEN
A Fresh Start

"Your work has been excellent so far, Mr. Parker. I'm very pleased," said Mr. Branson. Jonathan Branson was Christopher's new boss at Branson Software Engineering. Nearly seven weeks had passed since his discharge from Watermeadow. Fortunately for him, one of this father's engineering contacts came through.

"Thank you for giving me this opportunity, sir. Honestly, I can't thank you enough. But please, just call me Christopher. I always think of my father as Mr. Parker."

"Okay, Christopher it is then. I hope you'll be very happy here."

"Thank you, I've been happy so far, and I feel pretty certain it'll continue," making a conscious effort to smile.

"I'm glad. Well, it seems like the end of the day is here already, so I hope you have a good night and a great weekend."

"Same to you, Mr. Branson. I'll see you on Monday. Goodnight."

Christopher left the office for home, needing to shower and change his clothes as he was meeting Susan and her new boyfriend, George, for dinner that evening. He was expecting them to be swinging by his apartment at 7:00pm to be picked up for dinner.

He had a rather spacious apartment of two-thousand-square feet, that most considered to be quite a decent size for a single man living alone. What could he say? He inherited his parents' good taste and lavish lifestyle when it came to his home. The apartment had two large bedrooms, two full bathrooms, living room, library, gourmet eat-in kitchen with an island, and a generous formal dining room.

Christopher was treating Susan and George to dinner as a thank you for her continued friendship and the support she'd given him. More importantly, for remaining a loyal friend for all these years since high school, unlike many older friends who faded away when his alcohol abuse took over. He couldn't conceive his life without her being part of it.

Regarding her new-found beau, George, he found him to be everything she'd bragged about. He was kind, charming, handsome, funny, and he couldn't help but notice the family resemblance to his cousin, Jason. How he missed that man with a passion. He'd met the man for what was shy of two weeks, but he'd had such a significant impact on his life. Not just his physical health and emotional well-being, but the man had enriched his spirit for life itself. God, how he missed Jason's warmth, kindness, and not to mention the eye candy. The man had given him the kind of acceptance he thought was impossible, making him feel completely accepted, without judgment. The question one might ask was, did Christopher still want to date that man deep down? Fuck yes, he did! He had dreams during his sleep about Jason. Couldn't get the guy out of his head. How he hoped, at some point in the future, he could pursue that wish.

Bolting to the door when he heard the doorbell ring, "Come on in guys. I was just going to grab a light jacket for the evening. Seems a little on the chilly side, but I guess it won't be long till autumn gets here."

"You've such a magnificent apartment!" George said.

"Thanks—you're welcome to snoop around and take a self-guided tour." George wasted no time in taking him up on that offer, rapidly dodging around his home.

"That's because he's got his parents' expensive taste," Susan said loudly so George could hear her from whatever room he was now in.

"What can I say; she's right about me. It's who I am, I guess," Christopher said.

Calling out from the master bedroom, "Never apologize for having a beautiful home. Nor should you be sorry for your expensive taste. It's not a crime. Especially if you invite us over and allow us to enjoy the surroundings." George now rejoined the other two in the living room. "I guess we are ready to go on out to dinner."

"I agree, let's go. I've been looking forward to this evening all week. Getting to enjoy the company of two gorgeous men," Susan said with excitement.

Christopher giggled, "You're too much. The world would be far too boring without you in it to make it colorful."

"And don't you forget it!" she exclaimed. "Okay, let's get out of here already; I'm starving!"

In solidarity, Susan and George didn't touched alcohol when they were out with Christopher. He encouraged them to go ahead and indulge if they wished—that it wouldn't bother him one bit, but they wouldn't hear of it. And it wasn't as if they were big consumers of alcohol anyhow, so it didn't feel like they were giving up anything.

Susan picked the restaurant this evening, the Midwestern Steakhouse. She loved a great steak. Something she discovered that she had in common with her now boyfriend. Steak wasn't exactly Christopher's passion though, but this was his treat to them, so he had no problem going along with the choice of restaurant.

"So…," Christopher said with a long, drawn-out voice. "How's your cousin doing?" Trying not to sound nosy, but failing miserably.

Nodding his head in a nonchalant manner, George replied, "He's busy at work, of course. Not that there's anything new about that."

"Do you speak to him often?" he asked.

"Pretty often I'd say," George said with a determined voice. "We've been close for as long as I can remember. I can't picture life without him."

"That's nice, sounds like you two care a lot about each other."

"We love each other very much. I take it that you're starting to miss him?"

"Miss him!" Susan interrupted. "Boy—that's an understatement! I'd say *pining away* would be a better word choice."

Christopher tossed his hands in the air, "Okay, I confess! I'll admit it. I'm smitten with him."

"It's okay. No need to feel embarrassed about it," George said. "He knew you had a big crush on him."

"Oh my God!" Christopher exclaimed with astonishment, "He did? You mean he actually told you that?"

"Yes, he told me. It's not like he hasn't had patients crushing on him before. Typically, though, it's always been women. And I mean women of all ages. Truth be told, he's never had a patient develop a crush on him, who just so happens to be an eligible, attractive, gay man."

Christopher whined, "He's so goddamn good looking. It's no wonder the girls fawn over him. Hey—uh—did he actually tell you he thought I was attractive?"

"Oh, please! As if that would be a surprise to you!" George exclaimed and rolled his eyes. "Did he think you were attractive? Hmmm—what was it he said?" trying to recall Jason's precise words. "Oh, I remember now. 'The most beautiful, green-eyed male specimen I've ever laid eyes on'."

"Awwwww, that's sweet," he said in a soft voice.

"I gather you wish you could go out with him—on an actual date?" George asked.

"Gee, would I ever!"

"And I guess you're hoping he feels the same as you?" Christopher's head nodded to indicate a *yes* answer. "He's asked me about you to see how you've been doing."

Lighting up, "That's nice that he's thinking about me!"

"He's definitely thinking about you." George leaned across the table, in an attempt to get a little closer, "I've a tiny secret to share, if you'd like to hear it."

"Of course, I would," Christopher said with enthusiasm. "Tell me!"

"Well—what I think is that he's got a tiny little crush on you too."

"He does?" Susan and Christopher asked in unison.

"He really told you this?" she asked.

"No, he didn't say anything of the kind," George responded.

Christopher slumped over in disappointment, "Then how do you know?"

"Like with so many other things in life, it's what my gut feeling is telling me. I hear it in the tone of his voice, his facial expressions, his body language. He's a real professional though. He doesn't get involved with patients romantically. And since you were a patient of his, I feel like he won't let his heart go there."

"I always suspected Jason would take that sort of stance. The whole not getting involved personally with patients. I give the man a lot of respect for it. But...," he paused a moment. "I'm not a patient of his any longer."

"Susan and I agree, you're not a patient of his now. You're a terrific guy, and so is Jason. You both deserve the same happiness that we've found with each other. He wants to find a man to love so badly, I can't tell you how many times he's cried to me over it. But he's been burned so many times by bad relationships and learned so much from his past mistakes, he doesn't want to make the same mistake again." George said, trying to be sympathetic, "Tell you what. Let's give Jason—let's say—another six months. He needs to be convinced you're going to maintain your sobriety *and* stay that way. After all, most great things in life are worth waiting for."

"Yeah, that makes sense to me. I can appreciate his reluctance." Christopher couldn't disagree with George's line of thinking but hated the thought of waiting six more months.

"We'll figure something out—about setting you guys up together. Take out your cell phones, and we'll all mark our calendars for six months from now."

Once they determined the right date, they each put it on their respective calendars. "It's going to be a long six months," Christopher grumbled. "My poor balls will take on a permanent pastel shade of blue." Susan and George laughed hysterically. Eventually, Christopher couldn't help but join in. Once his laughter subsided, the expression on his face seemed more perplexed. "The one thing I worry about is that he might meet another guy during this time and fall for him instead of me."

George hunched his shoulders and responded to his concern, "I can't deny it's a possibility. A close friend of his, Peter, I think, convinced him to take a break from dating for a while, in the hope that sometimes, when you're not looking, the right person comes along. One thing I can tell you about Jason is that he's dated a whole lot of men. So many guys, I couldn't keep track of who he was dating at any given point in time. Anyhow, I'm hoping, that's where you'll come in. Maybe you can be the bachelor who shows up when he's not looking."

Christopher sighed with effervescence, "Like I heard in a Broadway show tune once, 'Wouldn't it be lovely'."

CHAPTER NINETEEN
Jason and George

The cooler, crisp air of autumn settled over the state of Indiana. Red, yellow, and orange foliage had taken over the once green landscape that once held such a stronghold during the months of spring and summer. It was two more months since Christopher made his transition into the world of sobriety. George and Susan were becoming ever increasingly etched into each other's lives, falling deeply in love with each other.

Christopher couldn't be happier for Susan for the love she'd found. She called him at least three or four days a week to report on her latest afternoon or evening she'd spent with George. And she left nothing to the imagination in the details of their romps in bed from the previous night. To the point Christopher was just a little uneasy at times around George, since he felt as if he knew more details of their sex life than anyone ought to have the right to know. But he wasn't going to squelch her happiness by telling her to hold back even if he knew she should.

George was so good, kind, and thoughtful to Susan, and for all the years she'd wanted Christopher on a romantic level, it gave him a deep sense of relief that she found so much joy in the arms of another man. A level of happiness she was decidedly entitled to and deserved.

Although he now discovered he had to share Susan's companionship with George. Still, that seemed a small price to pay. Albeit he was envious of the affection the two lovebirds shared, but he wouldn't have dared, for a second, to let either one of them know of the emotions he was concealing.

George was an absolute doll, and Christopher became quite fond of him. He was a huge fan of basketball, and Susan was way too dismissive of team sports of any kind. So, she would tell him, "Take Christopher with you. I'll only be bored to death! You'd be much better off going with someone who will actually enjoy watching the game with you." She knew already how much Christopher loved basketball, baseball, and hockey. And Christopher wasn't shy about telling George how he especially loved watching basketball because the uniforms showed the players bodies off the best. George would laugh over it, but he did enjoy Christopher's company. Thus, her two favorite men bonded pretty tight.

George could clearly see why she had been so attached to him since high school. What was hard for him to comprehend was that Christopher was, in fact, a recovering alcoholic. Since he was never exposed to him at his lowest point, to an extent, he was kept in a state of naivete. Susan told him he should consider himself blessed to have missed those god-awful years when this man, her closest friend on the planet, was a complete, fucked-up mess.

It happened on a Friday evening, that Susan flew to Seattle, Washington, to assist with a wedding she planned for the daughter of one of her best clients. The Brinkman's daughter, was marrying a man whose family was from Seattle, and she decided the wedding was to take place in the city that was to be her new home. As a result, George found himself alone for the weekend, and he couldn't stand the solitude. He begged Jason to spend the evening with him, not that he had to beg very hard.

Jason darted from the kitchen of his condominium to open the front door as soon as he heard the doorbell ring. "Come on in," he greeted George, giving him a tight hug. "I'm in the kitchen making dinner. Please help yourself to a drink. Just open the refrigerator and take whatever you want."

"Thank you. God, it's good to see you," he said, grabbing a Coke.

"Great to see you too, considering you don't give me the time of day since you've been dating Susan."

"Come on, Jason—that's not true! Is it?" George asked with a tinge of guilt in his voice.

"Well—I might be acting a little on the hyperbolic side." Shaking his head from side to side, "Gee whiz, you must be getting laid more often than a bricklayer's bricks." George immediately blushed hard. "My god! You're beet red! Apparently, I wasn't exaggerating on that point."

Being rather bashful, "Yeah—guilty as charged. But I *still* love you."

"And why wouldn't you? I was the one who fixed you guys up! Now you're getting as much pussy as you could possibly want. Meanwhile, I've gone so long without dick that I don't think I remember how to give a proper blowjob!"

George smirked and cocked his head, "I somehow doubt that. I'm sure it's like riding a bike. It'll come back to you."

"Hmmm—you think so, huh?"

"I don't personally have the same experience as you, but yeah, I'm fairly certain." Jason cracked a smile at George's remarks. "See, I speak the truth. Something smells awfully good. What's for dinner?"

"Spaghetti and meatballs," Jason replied. "Without much time to prepare an involved dinner, it was easy enough to boil spaghetti from a box and sauce from a jar. The meatballs are from the grocery store freezer. That delicious aroma you smell is the garlic bread baking in the oven, also from the grocery freezer section."

"As long as I'm sharing the meal with you, it'll be the best spaghetti and meatballs I've ever had."

"You *are* sweet! I do love you," said Jason.

"Of course, you do—and I can't thank you enough for fixing me up with Susan. I've never been happier." George leaned forward and gave Jason a quick kiss on the cheek.

Emotionally touched by the kiss, Jason smiled, "You're welcome. Have a seat. Let me make you a plate." Once the two men were sitting in the dining room eating, Jason asked, "Hey, tell me, how's Christopher Parker doing?"

"He's doing wonderful. I can't even comprehend how that guy ever had a drinking problem. I've become pretty attached to him. He's very happy with his new job as a software engineer. Damn! He's smart! Has this amazing apartment! It's huge! Beautifully decorated. Whatever you did for him, you turned him into a new man. His parents are elated. Susan is elated. You gave her back her Christopher."

"That's so good to hear. I truly felt he would be an enormous success. I'm so happy for him. I wish my entire case load was that successful." Jason's eyes puddled with tears.

"Hey—why are you crying? You must really care about him."

"The guy had some tough life history he had to put behind him. I care about all my patients. But you're right. Something is special about him. When you're that young and you can put your life back together—it's a real accomplishment. Now he's got his whole life ahead of him. Good for him!"

"You do excellent work, Jason. You do excellent work. Have—you—talked to your mom lately?"

He sighed and shook his head in a negative manner, "No."

"You're still so full of anger towards your mother."

"Yes—I know I am," he said sounding despondent.

"What's it going to take?" George asked.

Raising his eyebrows, "I'm not sure. I'm really not sure."

"Well, I'm always here for you. You know I love you."

"I know. I love you too. You've been more than a cousin to me. I always appreciate you spending time with me."

"Anytime. You know, I was the one who didn't want to be alone tonight. So, I should be thanking you."

"True. In that case—you're welcome."

CHAPTER TWENTY
Unexpected Coffee Date

F our more months passed by, and the city of Indianapolis was now in the grips of winter. The sad news was that the city was suffering a colder than usual winter with higher than average snowfalls. This reality made Christopher's hatred of winter that much more intense. He was miserable! However, the good news was that George and Christopher came up with a simple scheme to arrange a blind date for Jason. It was all quite easy. George explained to Jason he'd met a gentleman through his business contacts, who was looking for a fix-up. This so-called, nonexistent gentleman, was a gay man, and George just happened to know an eligible gay bachelor, his cousin, and it made for the perfect scheme.

They chose Christopher's favorite Starbucks as the backdrop for the blind date on the Saturday. Jason was arriving at 1:30 in the afternoon and would be wearing a navy corduroy blazer to make him recognizable. The blind date would be dressed in a green turtleneck and sweater to make him stand out as well. Everyone always told Christopher that wearing green would bring out the color of his eyes. The deception behind the plan was that Jason had no idea it would be Christopher he was actually meeting.

Christopher, albeit nervous, showed up at the Starbucks just a few minutes later than the 1:30 time slot, hopefully ensuring that Jason would be waiting for his date to show. Just as planned, he was sitting quietly with two cups of coffee in hand. George had suggested he arrive a tiny bit early and buy both cups of coffee, to make him the perfect gentleman. Having him come to Starbucks a little ahead of time, further added to the insurance factor that he'd be the one waiting for the date to arrive.

"Hi, Jason," Christopher said bashfully.

Looking up from his seat, "Oh, my God! Christopher Parker! What a sweet surprise! It's so nice to see you, and you look better than ever. You know, I'd love to sit and chat, and get caught up, but I'm actually expecting a blind date right now."

"Yeah—uh—well—how do I say this? It's me. I'm your blind date. Please forgive me for the deception. I know what you must be thinking. Why didn't I just call you at work and ask you out on a proper date? But—I was afraid you would shoot me down right away."

Now that he was made aware of being duped, Jason smiled at his once former patient and said, "Please—sit down." Christopher collapsed immediately on to the chair, thrilled that the invitation had been offered. "So, you and George cooked up this little plot for me?" Scratching the side of his head and tapping the tips of his fingers on the table top. "George thinks the world of you. You've done so well for yourself. Great new job. He brags about your gorgeous apartment. And George and Susan seem to be hot and heavy. They turned out to be a terrific match for each other. I couldn't be happier for George."

"She's ecstatic to be with him, couldn't be happier! And he hasn't just been good for Susan; he's become a great friend to me."

"So, he tells me. I suspected you had a crush on me when you were at Watermeadow, so I'm not *entirely* surprised by this ruse. It's sort of sweet."

"Look—I was a complete mess when you saw me there. But I'm not the same person now. George and I felt I needed to prove to you I was going to maintain my sobriety. And you needn't worry about any substance abuse on my part. George knew you'd never risk getting your heart broken." Jason nodded in agreement. "So, here I am, the newly updated version of Christopher Parker, who's still hoping and praying that you'll find it within your heart to give me an actual chance and go on a real date with me."

"I hope this updated version of Christopher Parker still has some of the elements I found so endearing." Christopher smiled at hearing this as Jason continued. "The Christopher I remember was smart, witty, a little bashful, with a strong sense of morality, and he has one of the kindest hearts I have ever encountered." Jason looked into his eyes and melted, "You still have the most amazing green eyes I've ever seen."

Christopher smiled back, "They're kind of a secret weapon of mine."

"It's a very effective weapon." Leaning his right elbow on the table and the side of his face on his fist, "I love a guy with beautiful eyes." He gazed at Christopher, up and down, "It's not just your eyes, you're very attractive from head to toe." He suddenly felt puzzled, "And you find me attractive? I always feel I look a little nerdy."

"That's just it! I've a real weakness for nerdy-looking guys. Jason—you're the most beautiful man I've ever laid eyes on. I even remember the very first time you approached me at Watermeadow, I was so dazzled by your good looks, I got this huge hard-on right away."

Jason blushed, "Did you really? Have you had an eye exam recently? Perhaps you need glasses."

"My eyes are just fine! You're *amazingly* handsome."

"Okay, okay, already. You win, you win. I give. I'd love to go out with you, Mr. Parker."

Christopher's heart was ready to burst with happiness. Suddenly, it didn't matter how cold and snowy the weather was. Jason Calhoun gave him the most precious gift in the world. And the gift was so plain. It was just a small word. Yes. *He said yes!*

"Listen, I need to tell you something about me," Jason said.

"Sure, what is it?"

"I'm a little gun shy about dating you, but I want you to know why. You see, something I've come to terms with, is that I'm a *rescuer*. When I say that about myself, I'm referring to a personality trait. In the past, I've always fallen for guys who needed rescuing. I love being needed and helping others. I've always fallen for men who are a bit of an emotional mess *because* they needed me. Being needed like that sucks me in. The thing is, I've learned I need to be with a guy who's stable. Someone who doesn't need to be rescued. I'm sure that's why I chose this career. My patients need me, and I love being there for them."

"But, Jason, I don't need to be rescued any longer."

"I know that, sweetie. You went out into the world and gave it everything you had to give. You're what I'm always hoping for. I always felt in my gut you were going to succeed. I was right!" He paused, "Please allow me to be a little reserved in this dating process. I want to be more secure in my feelings, that it's going to work out between you and me—before jumping into bed. I don't want my heart broken again, nor do I want to hurt you."

"Look, new relationships are always a risk. You have to be willing to risk getting your heart broken, that is, if you wish to find happiness. I wish I knew some way around it. In other words—what I'm trying to say—is there's never a guarantee that any new person you start dating is going to work out. At least until you finally kiss that one frog which turns into a prince."

Sighing deeply and gesturing with his hands for emphasis, "You're right. You're right. And I'm willing to take that risk."

"Sex can wait. I understand what you want. You want something that's more than great sex. The kind of stuff that carries you through tough times."

Jason cracked a huge smile, "That's it. That's it exactly."

Christopher, being lighthearted and playful, said, "Just—try not to keep me waiting too long for the sex. I'll do my best to behave myself, but like I said, you're incredibly cute. So, when do we go out on our first proper date?"

Jason reached across the table to take his hand. "Well—it was my impression—that we're on a date right now."

The gentle touch of his hand turned Christopher into a pile of mush. A glow of undeniable euphoria washed over his face. "Oh, that's right. We *are* on a date."

CHAPTER TWENTY-ONE
Dinner Date

Jason and Christopher were now deeply engaged in conversation, sharing details about each other's likes and dislikes as well as favorite hobbies and passions. The good news was, Jason became increasingly more comfortable and less awkward about the fact this man was previously a patient. Knowing how fond George had become of Christopher, he could hear his voice in the back of his mind telling him, *please try to enjoy yourself and let down your guard. Just give this guy a chance. He's the frog you've been searching for, I promise you.* So, he did just that. After all, why not? If George went to all the trouble of concocting this false pretense to get him here on this 'so called' blind date, perhaps his cousin was right. Maybe Christopher could bring him all the joy and love he wanted from a mate.

However, the bad news was, he felt somewhat at odds considering how they first met. "I feel like I've a bit of an advantage on you, and it makes me feel sort of awkward," Jason confided.

"How do you mean?" Christopher asked with concern. *I thought everything was going so well.*

"Feels strange to me, since I know so much of your family background and your various life struggles, all because of our talks at Watermeadow. I know more than I should be allowed to on a first date."

"Please—don't think it bothers me in any way. I love the fact you have never placed any negative judgment on me. I'm not sure other guys would be as understanding, especially since you know the truth about me being a prostitute before. You're the only one who knows. I've *never* even told Susan. It's so humiliating to me that I can't even share it with my closest friend."

"I take it that you haven't confessed to George either."

"Are you kidding? Especially him! He's the first real friend I've made since rehab. Don't forget, I still have to keep the confidences of my former customers." He frantically searched for a euphemism, "I don't ever want anyone to ask me about who I—*entertained.*"

"I can empathize with that. I'm not one to judge, sweetheart. How can anyone who's a member of the gay community hold others in judgment. Haven't we been judged enough already just for our sexual orientation."

"Most definitely!" he exclaimed.

"Look— we all have a past. We all have emotional issues and baggage. I don't give a damn about the choices you made in your past life. The past is the past. I hope you also feel the same about the mistakes I've made."

"Unquestionably! I would never judge you for your past mistakes. It seems to me we are what we are today because we have both learned from them."

"Damn, you're smart! George brags about how intelligent he thinks you are. I always thought you were. I think intelligence is sexy."

"Well, if you think intelligence is sexy, how are you going to keep your hands off me."

"I never promised I was going to do that!" said Jason with amour in his voice.

"I love the sound of that. What did you have in mind?"

"We can play it by ear. Listen, I'm getting hungry, and we've been here for several hours. Pizza is my favorite food, and my favorite

Pizzeria is just around the corner. Let's have dinner. My treat. What do you think?"

"Dinner with you? I feel like I just won the lottery."

They both stood up and layered on their heavy winter coats to brave the cold outside. Jason took Christopher by the hand, and he led the way to the *Pizza Kitchen*.

"This pizza is crazy delicious!" Christopher said. They had opted to split a large pepperoni and sausage pizza. "I've never been here before. I've seen this Pizza Kitchen driving by, but it looks like a real dive from the outside."

"Oh, I know, but like they always say, don't judge a book by its cover. This place is wicked delicious! Um—changing the subject, about what I was talking to you back at Starbucks. Is there anything about me you'd like to ask? No holds barred—whatever you want to know, go ahead."

"Gosh, I'm not in any kind of rush to find out every last detail about you. Although—I do have one question I'm curious about."

"Oh yeah, what's that?"

Being bashful, Christopher shyly asked, "A little bird told me you had a crush on me but never admitted it. Is that true?"

"Hmmm, a little bird told you. Any chance that little bird goes by the name of George?"

Continuing his goofy charade, "I'm just not all that sure anymore. The winter cold and snow seem to have frozen my memory."

He pondered the question, "You remember Judy, the nurse I work with at Watermeadow?"

"Sure, I remember her. Why? What does she have to do with the question?"

"*She* told me I had a crush on you, or at least that's what she saw. I'm guessing, if George felt the same way, something tells me I must have been giving off that kind of a vibe." Jason closed his eyes in deep thought and wrinkled his brow. "I suppose—being brutally honest with myself—the answer is yes. Yes, I did feel some affection towards you. Your personality and sweetness tugged at my heart." He chuckled, "That and those gorgeous eyes of yours. I suppose they were both right."

"Wow—that makes me feel special."

"You *are* special, trust me, you have no idea."

"Thank you. That means a lot to me," Christopher smiled.

Jason took a big bite of pizza and wiped his mouth with a napkin. "I love this stuff! So, is there any other burning question you have for me?"

"Let's turn that question around. Is there anything you feel is important that you feel you should share with me?"

"Yikes! That's a great question," he puzzled and scrunched his face. "Perhaps, just one thing comes to mind."

"Go on," Christopher encouraged.

"I lost my father when I was seventeen-years old."

Christopher felt bad immediately, "Jason, honey, I'm so, so sorry. How hard that must have been at such a young age."

"It's like I told you, we all have emotional baggage of some kind."

"If you don't mind, can I ask what happened? What took your father's life at what I assume was an early age?"

Jason looked at him squarely in the face. "He died from alcohol abuse. I had a rough childhood, having to cope with him being drunk so often. He was a mean son-of-a-bitch when he was drunk. All I could do was pray for him to get sober at those times."

Christopher reached across the table to hold his hand. Taking in a deep breath and letting it out slowly, Jason said, "So, now you know why."

"You mean, why you went into chemical dependency therapy?"

"That's right," Jason said while shrugging his shoulders. "I couldn't save my father, so I keep trying to save everybody else. Very often *without* success. That's why you're so special to me." His eyes filled with tears. "Oh hell, I didn't mean to start crying on our date." He grabbed a handkerchief from his pocket to dry his eyes.

"Don't apologize for showing emotion," said Christopher.

"Thank you, it's nice to have someone else on the listening end for once."

"For what you have done for me, I'm more than happy being here for you. It's the very least I can do."

"Thanks. Hey, how about we go back to your apartment after we're done eating. I want to see this place George brags about."

"Sure, that sounds fine with me. We can walk back to our cars, then follow me back to my place."

"Sounds great!" Jason said.

CHAPTER TWENTY-TWO
Christopher's Apartment

C hristopher fumbled with the keys to the front door of his apartment, as his hands were numb from the bitterly cold wind chill. "I hate this kind of fucking insane cold! This winter has been a bitch." He finally managed to get the front door open. Once they entered, he took Jason's coat and blazer and hung them up with his in the front closet. Then he raced to his living room, where he had a gas fireplace and flipped the wall switch to warm up the room. A cozy fire would provide the evening with a heightened romantic ambiance as well as additional warmth. He sought to be the consummate gentleman.

"Oh, my God! Your place is beautiful. I thought I had great taste, but this place blows me away. Your colors! Your artwork!" Christopher gave him a fully escorted tour around his home. "Good heavens, this apartment is enormous! I can see now that George wasn't exaggerating at all. This must be more than eighteen-hundred-square feet."

"Actually, it's two-thousand-square feet to be precise," Christopher proudly said. "I love it here, and being truthful, since it's large, it gives me a tremendous amount of storage space. All too often, apartments are so tight on that."

"You're not kidding! My condominium doesn't have half the storage space I'd like."

Trying to strike up some conversation, but not exactly being successful, Christopher said awkwardly, "So—um—would you like something to drink?"

"Do you have a diet soft drink?"

"Sure thing," pointing towards his couch in the living room, "Have a seat over there and make yourself comfortable. I'll join you in a minute."

Jason took a seat on the sectional sofa thinking *this looks like it could fit five or six guests*. Christopher brought out two glasses of Diet Coke and placed them on coasters on an adjacent coffee table. Jason tapped his hand on his lap, "Sit down here with me. I thought we could cuddle," he said wearing a big smile.

Christopher didn't need a second invitation. Down he went right next to Jason and slipped into his waiting embrace. He could vividly remember how wonderful it felt just to hug this man, and how he never wanted it to end. Cuddling with him on the couch was tantamount to a dizzying state of euphoria. Jason softly caressed Christopher's arms, who leaned his head into Jason's left shoulder. Jason tenderly cupped his fingertips underneath his chin and then raised his face upward, so he could stare deeply into his new lover's eyes. Always having found another man's eyes to be one of the sexiest features, the pools of emerald green behaved like an aphrodisiac intensifying his amorous instincts.

"Susan used to love staring into my eyes. Not so much now, with George around. But I've been so happy for her, and that's how it should be."

Nodding his head as a response, "I don't mind taking over that role."

Christopher allowed himself to be swallowed up by Jason's warmth and beauty. "You're hired." Feeling awestruck, "Part of me can't believe you're actually here."

"I'm really here. If this was part of some master plan, which apparently George helped you to conspire, I've taken the bait. So far, I'm glad I did." Jason caressed his face, relishing the feel of his dark, rough stubble. Christopher's five o'clock shadow was working its magic on Jason's arousal. He pressed his soft, warm lips to Christopher's, falling under the spell cast by the taste and feel. It had been a long, dry spell for both of these men, even if it had been by choice. Jason continued to press soft kisses from Christopher's mouth to his cheeks, and continuing a pathway down his neck and under his chin. The coarse texture of his beard continued to inflame Jason's libido. He finally turned his attention back to Christopher's hungry mouth and allowed their tongues to glide gently together.

Christopher's hands began drifting over Jason's torso while continuing to enjoy the deep and passionate French kissing. His hands drifted southward in their pursuit of Jason's below-the-belt treasure. It was as if his hands had a mind of their own, and he wasn't even conscious of his amorous efforts. Eventually, their pursuit paid off by the feel and heft of Jason's erection, which was grossly obvious, even if shielded by his trousers.

Jason suddenly inhaled deeply, separating their wet lips just enough to provide access to air. Christopher continued his assault by using his index finger to apply a light massage to the underside of Jason's dick. In response, Jason immediately used his hand to locate Christopher's erect member, and once found, he began a squeezing motion through the fabric of his pants. Slight moans of pleasure began to slip from both the men's larynxes.

At last, Jason broke away from the exquisite taste of Christopher's lips to catch his breath. "Hey, sweetheart, we'd better take it easy. If we keep this up, we're going to wind up in bed. I'm not quite ready for that yet, remember. But I do love what you have hiding in your pants. Damn! That's nice."

"Sorry, I guess I got carried away," Christopher said.

"You have nothing to be sorry about. It's all good. It isn't as if it's not noticeable that I'm truly enjoying myself."

For once, Christopher wasn't bashful, staring down at the undeniable bulge in Jason's pants. "Yeah—I'd say that huge boner of yours has blown your cover."

Jason laughed, "I must say you're right, there's no denying it." Just then, his cell phone buzzed with the notification of an incoming text message. "I apologize, I need to check my phone just in case there's an emergency. I'm actually on-call."

"Sure thing. I understand."

Upon looking at the text message, he broke into laughter and shrugged, "It's my friend Peter, and apparently, he's texting from his wife's phone. His wife is my friend Jennifer. She's one of my oldest friends from college."

Being curious, Christopher asked, "What's so funny? Is it important?"

"It's important to him I suppose. He's trying to find out how my date with you went. Apparently, he's under the impression that I must be home by now."

"Oh, I see. So, what are you gonna tell him?"

Jason grinned, "The truth. I'm going to text him back and tell him, 'We're making out on the couch right now and you're interrupting us'."

Now, Christopher's phone went off with the same ping of an incoming text message. "Now this is just too funny."

"Why? Who is it? What does it say?"

"It's George, he's texting me from Susan's phone, and he's also trying to find out how the date went."

"Oh, what a hoot! He's really gotten attached to you, hasn't he?"

"Yep, we're pretty tight. Hey, what should I text him back?"

Jason ecstatically said, "That's easy, tell him the same thing, 'you're interrupting our make-out session.' That'll give those guys something to gossip about."

The boys then placed their phones down on the coffee table and resumed their extended kissing session. Once the kissing cooled down, the two men continued to enjoy holding each other. Jason sat up for a second to look at the time on his cell phone. "Oh heavens! It's already 1:30 in the morning. I really ought to get going." But he groaned, "I hate going out in that horrible, bitter cold at this late hour."

"You're welcome to stay here for the night. I've a king-size bed to share."

"Oh, honey, I don't know. I'm not sure we'd be able to control ourselves in bed together. A great-looking guy next to me in the same bed. That may be more challenging than I can handle."

"Well, I do have a guest room if you're certain you can't resist my charms, but I think we can behave ourselves if we try. I would love the extra body heat on a wintry night like this. We can just cuddle."

Jason said, "Well, okay—it's against my better judgment. But honestly—I'd love to spend the night here with you. It'll be nice having a warm body to cozy up to."

The two boys went ahead and retired to the master bedroom. Shedding their clothes, but keeping their undergarments on for the warmth as well as in an attempt to hold off on sex for now. Not that either one of them were fooling themselves. Underwear and a T-shirt offered little protection, but they allowed themselves to fall into the trap of rationalization.

Once under the covers, they held each other for the shared body heat. However, due to the extended day in which they indulged themselves, they were finally consumed by exhaustion and fell into a very deep, contented slumber.

CHAPTER TWENTY-THREE
Early Morning

Jason and Christopher, as the expression goes, were both 'out like a light' for most of the night. Approximately, an hour prior to dawn, Jason repositioned himself in bed and cracked his eyes open. Looking around the bedroom to assess the time, he spotted a clock on an adjacent nightstand, which indicated that it was 6:05 in the morning. Not that he was in any mood to get up quite yet, but he did want to get a sense of what time it was. To the right of him, Christopher was sleeping heavily, and apparently, was decidedly a side sleeper. Beginning to miss the affection from the prior evening, Jason wanted to snuggle up by resting his head on Christopher's chest. He grasped along his left flank and gently tugged with the goal to reposition Christopher onto his back. Unfortunately, Jason learned quickly that Christopher had a tendency to startle easily.

"What—What's wrong?" Christopher sprang to life in a state of alarm. "Is everything all right?" Although Jason felt bad that he'd frightened him as much as he had, it did, however, achieve the desired effect of turning him onto his back.

"I'm sorry, sweetheart, I didn't mean to scare you." Not letting this desirable opportunity get away, Jason immediately swooped his head under Christopher's left arm and rested his head on his left upper chest. Then moving his left hand up as well so he could caress Christopher's right nipple, albeit through the white cotton fabric. "I started to miss you and wanted to snuggle."

"You were missing me? Aren't you the flatterer, considering I'm only inches away from you." Christopher used his arm to pull Jason in for a tighter embrace.

Continuing his flirtatious charade, "It was too many inches."

"Oh, you poor baby, we wouldn't want that," Christopher cooed. "I could so easily get used to this, waking up next to you every morning."

"Me too." Jason allowed his left hand to drift southward to sensuously caress Christopher's legs. The texture of his coarse, dark hairs triggered a primal sense of coziness and comfort. To Jason, body hair screamed masculinity and hairy legs were always a definite turn-on. The female form wasn't capable of providing the high, which enveloped him now. He loved the intimacy of cuddling with another man. In some ways, he enjoyed this simple intimacy even better than sex. In Jason's mind, this type of sensuous, intimate caressing would provide a prolonged romantic pleasure. With the engagement of sexual activity, the pleasure fizzled out after an orgasm was reached. Not that Jason was different from anyone else of the male gender. The pleasure his penis gave him on its journey to climax was an enjoyment he would never tire of.

Jason's hand traced up along Christopher's legs past his waist to slip it under his T-shirt. Suddenly, the touch and feel of abdominal and chest hair tantalized his fingertips. His fingers tenaciously combed through the forest of chest hair. Christopher fell into an abyss of relaxing pleasure as his chest hairs sent signals to his brain. "Oh, honey, this feels amazing. Please don't stop."

"Fuck! This is nice. I love hairy chests and yours feels like a deep pile carpet."

"I'm glad you like it," he said with an erotic tone. Chest hair behaved like an extra strength Viagra pill to Jason, sending his libido into overdrive. Without thinking, he slid his hand down under the waistband of Christopher's boxer briefs. His fingertips grazed through the thick bush surrounding Christopher's hardening dick. Jason's penis engorged rapidly with blood as his arousal began to peak and pressed against Christopher. "Damn! That's some monster you have down there," Christopher said.

Jason began tugging gently on Christopher's rigid cock, causing soft murmurs of pleasure. Despite his enjoyment, Christopher came to his senses, "Wait, honey, wait." Jason ceased his assault on Christopher's hard shaft. "You said you didn't want to do this. Please let's not do something you might come to regret." Not wanting to hurt Jason's feelings, "Sweetheart, please don't get me wrong, I love that you find me attractive. It's a *wonderful* feeling. And my hard-on isn't hiding my attraction for you either. But I know you want a real relationship, and you want to be sure I didn't just want to get into your pants. I want the same things you do. Of course, I'd be lying if I didn't confess that I'm *dying* to get into your pants. But that's just my hard-on talking. Still, I would much rather wait until you feel completely secure. This is far too important to me to fuck this up."

Jason moved his hand back up to Christopher's upper chest, an apparent safe zone, softly palpating his right nipple again through the T-shirt. "You're right. I know you're right. That's exactly what I want. I really like you. I like you a lot. Yesterday was the most amazing time I've had in I don't know how long. I feel so completely comfortable around you. And for whatever reason, my gut tells me I can trust you. I've never felt this way about a guy before."

Christopher pulled Jason into an even tighter embrace. "Thank you. I've dreamed about you for so long. Always wanting this, but never sure if I could ever have you by my side."

"I understand, and I'm incredibly grateful to have fallen into the web you and George spun for me. The thing is, right now, please I'm begging you. I'm so fucking horny and my dick is aching for release," Jason pleaded.

Christopher sighed, "Are you absolutely sure you want to do this? No regrets?"

Looking right into his eyes, Jason replied, "I've never been more sure about anything."

Christopher smiled in the dark, "Okay," and he turned Jason onto his back. Then grabbed the bottom of Jason's T-shirt and pulled it off over his head. He followed up by pulling his underwear off under the blanket and sheets. Christopher began deep, passionate French kissing with Jason. The taste of his tongue sent a rush of blood to his own cock making it rigid again. While caressing his left nipple, he made the discovery that he wasn't the only one in bed with a treasure trove of chest hair. Afflicted by the same weakness, he combed through Jason's chest hair and let his hand glide southward, tracing the happy trail to his waiting, massive erection. Once he'd taken a firm grasp of it and began a slow massage, he moved his lips down the length of Jason's neck and settled on his left nipple, gently kissing and drawing it into his mouth to suckle, but continuing slow deliberate strokes on Jason's penis.

With continued pleasuring of his partner, Christopher repositioned himself on top of Jason with his lips pressing kisses into Jason's navel. The kisses traveled downward into Jason's thick pubic hair until at last, he was pressing his lips to the head of Jason's cock. He licked all around the head and then let his tongue glide into his slit, savoring the taste of a man for whom he'd starved himself from for many months. Finally, he took the entire length of Jason's manhood into his mouth, letting his lips glide up and down the stiffened length and enjoying this with as much pleasure as he was giving. He cupped and softly caressed Jason's heavy balls, creating louder gasps of pleasure, and the faint taste of precum hit his tongue. Jason's balls began to tighten and draw upward, alerting Christopher to his pending orgasm. But he was having far too much fun and didn't want this session to end so quickly. As soon as he could tell from Jason's respirations that his orgasm was imminent, he used his thumb and index finger to encircle the base of Jason's erection. Then tightened his grip firmly preventing Jason's climax.

Jason's sexual pleasure and breathing calmed, but his erection remained solid. Once Christopher was assured he prevented his ejaculation, he wasted no time in restarting his cock-sucking action to extend Jason's erotic pleasure. As heavier flows of precum leaked from Jason's dick onto his tongue, he slowed the up and down sucking action and lessened the friction his mouth was providing. Thereby extending the relentless pleasure he was giving to Jason. By this point, Christopher's cock began to drip his own precum, and his head became dizzy with his own sexual arousal.

Once again, Jason's balls tightened upward, and he knew his partner was coming very close to the point of no return. He repeated pinching off Jason's climax and waited for him to exhibit signs that he had been rescued from falling off that cliff.

Christopher saved his most pleasure-giving treatment until last. He cradled Jason's engorged, leaking cock in his right hand, allowing him to access the underside. Then, beginning at the base, he traveled up the entire length of Jason's penis, lashing with soft flicks of his tongue, from side to side, relentlessly but with minimal friction. Doing everything possible to hold off Jason's climax. Once he reached the top of the underside, just below the head, and armed with the knowledge of how intensely pleasurable it was, to lick around that region, he persisted on his goal of providing Jason his long-awaited orgasm. He kept his tongue moving slowly to keep edging Jason into pure ecstasy, always careful to provide the lightest friction. When his balls started to clench up again, Jason started pleading, "Don't stop. Please I'm begging. Please keep going." Jason's body stiffened up, and his respiration became labored while climbing to orgasm. At last his large, hard dick erupted in repeated spasms with cum spurting over his chest and abdomen.

Eventually, Jason's labored breathing calmed, and he returned to a world of consciousness. "Oh—my—fucking—God! That was amazing." Christopher repositioned himself in bed so he could reach into the top drawer of the nightstand, grabbing a clean, white washcloth, which served the purpose of a 'cum rag.' He sponged away the semen from his lover's chest and belly region. Despite the darkness, he could easily use his sense of touch with the tips of his fingers to detect the familiar spots of viscous fluid. He sifted through Jason's body hair, paying particularly close attention to the bush surrounding his softening penis, since he knew that area would generally catch more than its fair share.

"I thought you'd enjoy that special treatment," Christopher said, pleased with himself.

"Did I ever! Flip over so I can have a turn at giving you the same pleasure. Now I know all your secret weapons," Jason said eagerly. "Keeping me from coming—that was wicked! But it felt fantastic."

The boys reversed positions, and Jason delivered the same, exact waves of erotic excitement, making certain to keep in tune to the telltale signs of Christopher's pending orgasm. Just before he was about to explode, Jason staved off his release in the same fashion. He threw in one wrench. He wouldn't allow Christopher to reach a climax on the third round. No, he still made him wait.

Jason used that same technique of the soft flicking of his tongue on the underside of Christopher's pulsing cock. Always careful to lick with the lightest touch so he could edge him into a sexual frenzy. Jason took the head of Christopher's erection into his mouth, firmly surrounding his lips around the tip. This still allowed Jason full use of his tongue gliding softly from side to side on the underside of the head, all the while knowing the pool of pleasure he was supplying.

Christopher's balls, while being fondled began their climb upward no-
tifying Jason that his ejaculation was yet again, imminent. As antici-
pated, Christopher began pleading for his orgasm, "I need to cum,
please, Jason, you need to let me cum."

Jason wasn't going to torture him any further. His entire body
quaked with pleasure. At last, his tongue had achieved its goal, and
Christopher's penis exploded with an intense, massive orgasm. Since
Jason still had his lips wrapped securely around the head, the ejaculate
spilled directly into his mouth, and he swallowed creating minimal
clean up. Although Jason enjoyed the lack of cleanup, he didn't kid
himself, not at all. For some unknown primal reason, he greatly enjoyed the sensation of his partner's orgasm flooding his mouth.

Both men, now sexually satiated and sleepy, slipped back into
their favorite cuddle position. Before they drifted off to sleep, Jason
suddenly remembered he'd made a brunch date. "Hey, it just hit me, I
made a date with my friends, Jennifer and Peter Berringer, this morning."

"Wasn't Peter the friend who was texting you last night?"

"That's him. Would you like to come with me, please? I'm sure
they won't mind. I'm supposed to be there at 11:30. I can send them a
text to let them know. They're such great friends of mine. Would you
come, pretty please?"

"Sure, if you'd like me to join you. Sounds like fun, and it means
we can spend more time together."

"Thank you, sweetheart. You're so wonderful!" Jason leaned over
to give Christopher another kiss on the lips. "I do need to run by my
place just to change my clothes though. I guess I can shower here first."

"Are you kidding? After that *sensational* blowjob, shit, I'm ready
to let you move in if I can wake up to that every day."

"Awwwww—thank you—and you're welcome." Their sexual release took its toll and they drifted back to sleep.

CHAPTER TWENTY-FOUR
Sunday Brunch

The two men arrived at the front door of the Berringer's. "Welcome, guys, please come in," Peter said after opening the front door. He embraced Jason and squeezed him tightly with the same warm hug he'd always expect. But being less familiar with Christopher, extended his arm for a handshake, "It's a real pleasure to meet you. Glad you could join us."

"Thanks so much for having me," Christopher said, making sure to appear gracious.

Jennifer appeared from the kitchen to greet their guests, exchanging kisses, hugs, and handshakes as appropriate.

"Oh, I'm so sorry, where are my manners," Jason said, realizing that he hadn't provided a proper introduction. "Guys, this is my boyfriend, Christopher Parker." Redirecting his attention, "Honey, do you remember last night, I mentioned Jennifer and I met during college."

Did I just hear right? Did he just introduce me as his boyfriend?

"We're so happy to have you both." Susan said to Jason, "I have to tell you, at the risk of embarrassment, your boyfriend is *very cute!*"

Christopher immediately felt choked up with joy inside; his heart burst with so much emotion, that his eyes partially filled with tears. *He did! He called me his boyfriend. I can't believe it. I'm actually somebody's boyfriend!* Jason looked happily at Christopher, "I agree, he's crazy cute!" But then noticed the tears puddling in his eyes. "Honey, what's wrong? Did we say something to upset you? Why are you crying?"

"Sorry—I'm not upset," using his hands to wipe the tears away. Trying to speak now with a lump in his throat. "I'm not upset over anything. It's just that, in my entire adult life, no one has ever considered me to be their *boyfriend*. You can't imagine how nice it feels just to be given that status."

Jason smiled and leaned over to give Christopher a peck on the lips. "I'll always be proud to introduce you as my boyfriend."

Jennifer said to Peter, "That's so sweet. Isn't it, honey?"

"Yes, it is," he said with a look of pleasant surprise. "Honestly, I can't remember the last time I saw you this happy, Jason."

"Well, thanks. Okay, I'm starving. When do we eat?" Jason said.

Jennifer gestured with a directing hand, "You boys go have a seat in the dining room. I'll bring everything through from the kitchen. I have a frittata baking in the oven, which should be done momentarily."

The three men moved to the dining room and seated themselves. Peter wanted to apologize in the most delicate way possible, "By the way, I'm sorry about interrupting you guys last night with my texting. So, Jason, when *did* you finally get home last night?"

Jason stuttered with embarrassment, "Uh… well, um… You see… I didn't exactly…"

Right then, Peter burst into laughter, "You, dog you! You never went home, did you? And you swore to me that you could behave yourself and not jump into bed right away!" Tears filled his eyes from his uproarious laughter. "Apparently, your new boyfriend is not only cute, but he must have enough chest hair it resembles a rug!"

Christopher nudged Jason and whispered, "Did you tell him about my chest hair?"

Jason blushed, "Now, Peter, you're going to get me in trouble. You make it sound like I just used him for sex. And in my defense, we didn't have sex till this morning. So, give me a little credit."

"Holy shit! You waited till *this morning*?" As if he had made some huge sacrifice, Peter's laughter surfaced again. Once he could catch his breath, he said to Christopher, "Please accept my apologies if I said anything to embarrass you. I'm just giving your boyfriend a hard time. You should know, I absolutely love Jason like family. In truth, I would have to say *better* than family. He's the kindest—most generous—warmest man I know. Outstanding character! Aside from my wife, he's the person I enjoy spending time with the most. You know, there are few people in this world who can make you happy just from their presence. That's who Jason is." Changing his tone to something more playful, "I *know* what kind of guy turns his head. I love big tits, and he goes for chest hair." Gesturing by holding both hands up in the air, "It's just guy talk we have had, that's all. So, it was pretty apparent to me, if he slept with you so fast," he struggled to contain his laughter, "you must have gotten his dick so hard, it could cut diamonds." Peter collapsed into uncontrollable guffaws, making it difficult to catch his breath. Once he could regain his composure, he said, looking directly at Jason, "Am I lying?"

Jason finally confessed with bashful eyes, "No. It's all true."

"See how well I know him. Let me just say this. You're never going to date a more wonderful guy than Jason. I promise you, there's no man out there who will treat you better."

Bringing his voice down, close to a whisper, wishing to keep this from Jennifer's ears, Jason said to Peter accompanied by hand gestures, "It's true! I'm weak. I couldn't help myself. His body is so fucking hot! My dick could have cut something harder than diamonds. If such a thing existed."

Peter said with a mischievous smile and nodding, "As long as he makes you happy. That's all that matters to me."

Christopher leaned over towards Jason, "I like him! No wonder you're so crazy about Peter."

"He's a *really* good guy! And Jennifer is my oldest and dearest friend, not to mention she's a fabulous cook!"

Now a little worried, Christopher asked, "Are you sorry now that we had sex?"

Using a demonstrative voice, "Oh, hell no! I don't regret it for one second! I'm already looking forward to the next time."

"Well, it's not going to be in here," Peter said teasing.

Jennifer finally arrived in the dining room with a large gruyère, spinach, onion, and mushroom frittata, strips of bacon, and hash brown potatoes.

"Did I hear someone bragging about my good cooking?"

"As if you have to ask," Jason said. "It all looks delicious! I love you. Thanks, guys, for having us."

"We love you, too. You're such a sweetheart," Jennifer said smiling. She asked him, "Would you be an angel and help me bring in the croissants, coffee, and orange juice. Oh, and I guess we should bring back some coffee creamer."

"Sure thing," he answered.

As soon as Jennifer had gotten Jason alone to herself in the kitchen, she asked, "I can't help noticing, he has the most gorgeous green eyes."

"You know how I love sexy eyes."

"Yes, I remember well how you fancy beautiful eyes and they're stunning! Green eyes aren't so unusual, but you don't see that kind of—pale, kelly-green color. I'm terribly curious though. Didn't you say you had a patient a while ago who had these same remarkable green eyes?"

"Yes. That's him. And I know what you're probably thinking."

Jennifer gestured with her hands in a negative manner, "No, I'm not judging you. Not at all. Sweetheart, we've known each other for years. You're a very bright man, and I've complete faith in your judgment. So, how did you wind up going out with him."

"You know my cousin George?" Jason asked.

"Sure, I do. He's such a doll!"

"Yeah—he's a doll alright. Anyhow…" He proceeded to relay the story of George's friendship to Christopher and Susan, and how they planned the phony blind date.

"God bless him! He's done incredibly well for himself since his rehab then."

"He has indeed," he agreed.

"You know how I'm a big believer in fate. I can't explain it. I just feel life brought you two together for a reason. Come on, let's get all this food back to the dining room and dig in."

The rest of the spread was placed on the dining room table. Christopher was immediately impressed by her cooking. She was quite the gourmet. Great food, friendly conversation, and an enjoyable time were had by all four of them.

When it came time to depart, the two hosts gave each of them a hug and dispensed with the handshakes. Peter whispered softly in Jason's ear while they hugged, "I think he's the one." Jason winked back his acknowledgment when they separated from the embrace.

Christopher was touched by the couple's warmth and sincerity. He and Jason bundled up in their winter coats and took off. Once back in the car, he said, "I had a terrific time with them; such nice people and incredible food."

"They've been fantastic friends to me. Gotten me through some tough times. So, what do you want to do now?"

"Just what did you have in mind? You just don't want this date to end, do you?"

Freaking out a little, "Am I wearing out my welcome? I don't want to take advantage of you or your time."

Christopher said joyfully, "I love spending time with you. It's like being in a dream that I'm afraid to wake up from."

Giving him a kiss, "You're so romantic! Thank you for this wonderful weekend!" Jason asked in a frisky, affectionate, and playful manner, "Hey, we could go back to my place for some more great sex!"

Christopher wrinkled his brow, "After this morning's bedroom antics, I think my sexual batteries need a little time to recharge. How about we take a nap first. Especially, after that huge meal. You can have your way with me *after* we wake up."

"Hot damn! I can't wait till we wake up then." The two men pressed their lips together one last time before they drove away.

CHAPTER TWENTY-FIVE
The Invitation

Christopher and Jason were now a number of weeks into their courtship, and both the men couldn't be any happier. Their dating seemed to quickly evolve into what many would have termed, *serious.* They tried their best to see each other three or four days a week. And men being men, they had to see each other at least that often just to keep their sexual appetites in check. It was Friday afternoon, and Christopher was cooking dinner at his apartment for Jason. This was the first time he was cooking for his new beau, as his parents would put it, and he was eager to get out of the office a little early, so he could get a head start on preparation.

He knocked on Mr. Branson's office door. "Come in, please." Once inside the office, Mr. Branson asked, "Hey, Christopher. What can I help you with?"

"Would it be possible to leave thirty minutes early today? I could manage to leave at our regular ending time, of course, but I was hoping to get a little jump on a dinner engagement."

"Someone special I'm guessing?"

"I'd say that's very accurate. This person is quite special to me."

"Sure, that's not a problem You can go ahead and take off now if you like."

"Thank you, Mr. Branson. I do appreciate it."

"You're welcome. Oh, by the way, as long as you're here, and being that you're somewhat newer to my company, I wanted to give you a heads up that I'll be having our Annual Employee Appreciation Dinner in three weeks. I have it every year at the beginning of spring. It's a formal affair that I host at the Applewood Country Club. Of course, I'd like you to attend, and you should bring a date. Since I don't see a wedding band on your hand, I assume the special person you're referring to is a girlfriend who you can bring with you."

As if someone had just knocked the wind out of him, Christopher went lifeless inside. He'd spent so many years hiding his sexuality from his family, friends, as well as his coworkers during the periods of time when he was properly employed, he simply didn't know how to respond. Yes, he certainly wasn't a closet case anymore, but with his new employer, he was petrified. *Shit! What the fuck am I going to say now. I'm thrilled working here. But what if Mr. Branson has a problem with gay people? I don't want to lose this job. I can't lose this job! Jason isn't going to want an unemployed boyfriend, I'm damn sure of that.* Those same old tapes that played in his head suddenly resurfaced. All those years he spent living in his invisible closet, always trying to shelter the outside world from learning the truth about who he really was. How those mental tapes crippled him for so many years. Christopher forced a smile as much as he could, "Thank you for the invitation, I'll look forward to it. Goodnight."

He bolted out of the office to make a pit stop at the grocery store before heading home. He was missing some key ingredients he needed to complete his main entrée for dinner. This was the real reason why he wanted the thirty-minute head start.

Meanwhile, Jason was still finishing his day up at Watermeadow. He hadn't seen Christopher since Wednesday, and he was missing him something awful. Nurse Judy stopped by his office door, "I just wanted to say goodnight and wish you a nice weekend. Any special plans?"

"Yeah—Christopher is cooking me dinner tonight for the first time. I haven't seen him for forty-eight hours!" He lightheartedly exclaimed, "I'm getting desperate for my fix."

"Oh, heavens, has it been that long since you've seen your boyfriend? How have you survived so long without him?" She laughed aloud, "Oh my, you have it bad. I think someone is in love," she said in a whimsical tone. She smiled, "You have fun tonight. Take care." With that, she took her leave as she was off for the weekend and looking forward to some *me* time.

Jason's face took on that same familiar pensive look. Is it true? Am I in love with him? Who the hell am I kidding? I live day to day in a state of intoxication. He's all I seem to ever think about. If I didn't force myself to focus on my work here, I wouldn't get anything accomplished. I can't even stand being separated from him, even if it's for a day. If that's not love, what is? His heart swelled with joy, and he got that familiar lump in his throat whenever he felt emotional. Maybe I'm afraid that the relationship will go kaput as the others did? Shrugging his shoulders, it's true though; I do love him. Now I can't see my life without him. With his eyes becoming misty, all he wanted to do was hold Christopher in his arms.

Before he left his office for the night, right then, he felt he had to share these feelings. He had to tell someone this good news. Without hesitation, he knew right away who he wanted that someone to be. The one person who'd been there for him for a lifetime. He picked up the phone to dial out.

"Hello," came from the other end of the line.

"George, it's me, Jason," he said.

"Hey, how the hell are you? Seems like I haven't heard from you in forever. Or, in point of fact, since I fixed you up on that date with Christopher."

"I'm sorry I haven't called. I didn't mean to ignore you."

George smiled into the phone, "It's okay, I know you've been otherwise occupied," he said with a chuckle.

"Uhhh… What is that supposed to mean?"

"I must say, normally, I would've profusely apologized and begged your forgiveness for the deception I used on you." George continued trying to be cute and sarcastic at the same time, "However, from what Christopher tells me, how should I put this delicately, the two of you are *fucking* like rabbits! So, don't tell me you're not gettin' any!"

"That's your idea of delicate? That's putting it pretty bluntly I'd say. So… Ummm… Exactly how much detail is he sharing with you?"

George began to snicker, "Enough. I seem to recall several months back that you complained to me you had gone so long without dick… Oh heck. Let me think here. How did you put this?" He pondered for several seconds. "You said to me you thought you had forgotten how to give a proper blowjob. Do you remember that?"

Jason, becoming shy and reserved, "Uhhh… Yeah, I think I remember something like that. And your point is?"

Desperately trying to contain his laughter, "Christopher tells me that you are quite talented with your—uh— technique. Apparently, you haven't lost your edge." George collapsed into laughter over the phone.

"Okay now, you've had your fun." Jason knew right then George was teasing. Now he giggled at himself, "You were right though. It came right back to me. Oh my God, I can't believe he shared those kinds of details of our sex life. So, he really tells you I'm that good?"

"Are you kidding? From his perspective, you're an insanely talented lover. You have that man walking on air he's so gaga over you. And that's when you're *not* giving him blowjobs. If he's in the midst of receiving one, he's in a state of pure delirium. I'm telling you, he is completely ecstatic over you. Susan has never seen him this happy, ever."

Jason sighed with love in his voice, "Oh… That's so nice to hear. Still, I'm kind of embarrassed that he shared so much information with you."

"Excuse me! You're embarrassed the guy thinks you're *amazing* in bed? I understand why this might make you feel bashful. But, Jason, he's just trying to share his happiness with me."

"You're right. Point taken." Suddenly, realizing he had something else to worry himself over, "Has he told Susan all these graphic details as well?"

"I… I don't think so. He gushes on to her about how happy he is with you. And even though they're extremely close, I don't think he would feel so comfortable sharing *that* much information. Not with a woman. Men are much more comfortable talking about their sex lives with other men. You know what I'm talking about."

"Yeah, I catch your drift. George—I'm in love with him. I'm crazy in love with him!"

"I'm so happy for you! Really, that's the best news. And you deserve it."

Jason paused, "Although I haven't told him yet."

With painful curiosity, George asked, "Why not for God's sake?"

"I only realized just before I called you. He's all I can think about. I hate being away from him. All I want to do is hold him."

"Sounds like you're in love, alright. So, when are you going to tell him?"

"Tonight. I'm hoping he feels the same about me."

"That won't be a problem," George confirmed confidently.

"Why? Has he told you he's in love with me?"

"He doesn't have to. He reeks of euphoria. Susan agrees with me too."

"You think so, huh?"

"Yeah, I do." After a brief pause, George insisted, "Well—don't just sit there. Go to him."

"Okay, I'm leaving now. Bye."

"Bye, buddy. Hey, Jason?"

"Yes?" He asked back.

"I just wanted to say I love you."

"I love you too. Always have."

As soon as, Jason hung up the phone, he bolted from the office and drove over to Christopher's apartment just as fast as it was legal and let himself in. Christopher had already given him a key to his place.

"Hey, honey, I'm here," he announced. He found Christopher in the kitchen and tossed his arms around him and squeezed tightly. Then holding onto his face, he kissed him. Jason caressed his cheeks and looked at him with doe eyes. "I just love the way your lips taste."

He smiled back and furrowed his brow line, "Thank you. That's sweet of you to say and a little flirtatious."

Jason's nostrils flared out and inhaled deeply, "Something smells delicious! What is it?"

"It's called pastitsio. I also made us a salad to go with it."

"What is it? I've never heard of pastitsio."

"It's a pasta dish a lot of people will describe as a Greek lasagna."

"Oh, it's Greek then?"

"Yep, that it is. It's made with pasta shells, beef, lamb, tomatoes, cinnamon, Greek yogurt, parmesan cheese, onions, some heavy cream, garlic, eggs, and a little red wine. I know there's more ingredients than that, but that's what comes to mind right now. I can't make it without following the recipe carefully. Too many steps."

Jason suddenly frowned, "Red wine?"

"Honey, it's a cooking wine. It's loaded with salt. You can't drink that shit by itself. Tastes like garbage. Besides, don't you trust by now that I'm staying sober?"

Jason bobbed his head from side to side, "Yes, of course I trust you. I'm sorry, I shouldn't have said anything. Please forgive me."

Christopher gave Jason a kiss, "You're forgiven."

Jason inhaled deeply again, "It smells amazing!"

"Go sit down in the dining room, and I'll bring it right out. Oh, honey, would you grab the salad from the counter if you please," Christopher said while extending his index finger, gesturing towards the large bowl.

Christopher pulled the hot casserole dish from the oven and carried it out to the dining room table and set it down. The pastitsio was bubbling hot and steaming away. Being the perfect gentleman, he served his boyfriend first and then himself.

Taking a bite, Jason exclaimed, "Dear God, the taste is amazing! I'd no idea you were such a great cook."

"Well—I do have other talents than just my lovemaking. You seem to appreciate those as well."

Jason blushed slightly and reached over to caress his face again, using his thumb in a light sweeping back and forth motion, enjoying the rough feel of his beard. "Yes, I do." He cleared his throat, "I talked to George a little bit ago."

"Oh, and what did he have to say?" Christopher asked with curiosity.

"How much you enjoy the blowjobs I give you."

"Oh that," he said, now feeling guilty. "Sorry if I said more than I should. But—you're really good at it."

"So, I've been told. It's okay. I was quite a bit embarrassed at first, but George knocked some sense into me that I shouldn't be."

Feeling embarrassed himself now, "How did he do that?"

"It's not important right now. Sweetheart, there's something I need to tell you. And I do hope you feel the same way. You see, I've been so happy since we started dating, and the truth is, I hate being away from you. Whenever we're apart, all I ever do is pine away, wishing I was with you again."

He smiled back, "I feel exactly the same way. I hate being separated from you."

"Darling... I can't believe I just used the word *darling*. Oh geez, that sounds so sappy."

"I like sappy," Christopher smiled eagerly.

"The thing is, I'm in love with you. I can't see my life without you."

"I'm head over heels in love with you too. You've made my life..." Christopher was at a loss for words. "I can't think of an adjective special enough to use."

Jason reached across to grab another kiss. "I'm so glad you feel the same way. Now changing the topic to another pressing concern, sweetheart—have you told your parents about me? I've been a little worried about your mom and dad. About how they will feel about me, since I was your case manager at Watermeadow. I did meet them once you might recall."

"I told my parents a while back that I had a beau."

"Wow, you told them you had a *beau*. That's sweet."

"My parents taught me that word, *beau*. I'd never heard of that expression for a boyfriend before. They seem quite happy for me."

"Beau is a pretty old expression, that's for sure. But it's sweet. I like that, being your beau. I like that a lot. Still, did you tell them who your beau was?"

"Yes, I did, honey. They know exactly who I'm dating. I told them about my feelings towards you and how much I wanted you."

"And what did they say, specifically, your father?" Jason asked with trepidation.

"My father said he's not surprised. He knows that once I have my mind set on something, I do what I need to achieve the desired result. They'd love to meet you again."

He pondered, "Wow... Meeting the parents. That's a big step!"

"Uh—That brings up a question I've been meaning to ask you. I know about the loss of your father. Of course, you know how sorry I am about that. But... you haven't said a word about your mother. Why?"

Jason pursed his lips, took a deep breath, and sighed, "I don't have a good relationship with my mom, I'm afraid."

"What's wrong, Jason? You of all people, to have a poor relationship with your mother. That doesn't sound at all like you."

Jason took another bite of the pastitsio. "Honey, I'm very bitter and angry towards her. Frankly, I'm pissed at her for not removing me, her only child, from such a toxic father," he scowled. He whined, "I'm so envious of you and your relationship with your parents."

"Perhaps it's time to patch things up with your mom if you can. After all, she's the only parent you have."

"I'm certain you're right. It may be time to put the past behind me. I don't think I'm quite ready yet, still."

"Well, if you ever want to talk about it, I'm all ears." He took a few more bites of his dinner as he needed to summon some courage as well. "Sweetie, something came up today at work that I've become quite upset over."

"Go on," Jason listened intently.

"Mr. Branson invited me to the Annual Employee Appreciation Dinner and strongly encouraged me to bring a date."

"And? What's the problem? That's hardly an unusual invitation."

"Mr. Branson assumed I have a girlfriend."

"I see—that's not such an unrealistic assumption. Yes, it would be nice if people didn't make that assumption. Sweetheart, the fact is, most individuals are straight. That's just how the world is. I'm sure he didn't mean to offend you."

"I didn't tell him the truth. I didn't know what the fuck to say! I've spent so many years hiding in the closet, always afraid of rejection, I couldn't tell him the truth. Sometimes I'm still that scared fifteen-year-old, who's afraid of getting fired if my boss knows the truth about my sexuality. And I don't care what the laws say about discrimination against sexual orientation. If he wants to get rid of me, he can figure some other way to push me out the door. I love this job! I'm good at what I do."

Jason put his fork down and reached out to hold both of his hands in his. "Do you think that he'll fire you if he discovers you're gay?"

Christopher grimaced, "I really don't know. But I'm afraid to find out. And I won't deny that part of my concern is the fact you want a boyfriend who's employed. I love you so much, I don't want to lose you."

"Sweetheart, I'm not leaving you. And if you were fired due to the fact that your boss doesn't want a gay man for an employee, I wouldn't leave you over that either. That being said, you need to feel secure in your job and secure about your boss not letting you go over your sexual orientation. You drank yourself into oblivion over feelings of low self-worth for these kinds of fears. You don't know whether Mr. Branson will give a shit that you're gay. He hired you for your engineering skills and mathematical wizardry. You need to hold your head up high, be honest with him, and tell him that you'd like to bring your boyfriend to the dinner. Honestly, sweetheart, you're probably worried about nothing."

Hearing these words helped Christopher ease some of his fears. Although he knew he was somewhat frightened of approaching his boss. He also knew he had to face his anxiety head on, because that was the only way he could conquer it.

Jason gazed at his boyfriend with his doe eyes and took another bite of food. "So, um, how would you like a blowjob for dessert? Since I know how much you enjoy them."

"Sounds delicious." He sighed, "I love you, Mr. Calhoun."

Jason leaned over to steal another kiss, "I love you too, Mr. Parker."

CHAPTER TWENTY-SIX
Meeting the Parkers

Saturday morning greeted Jason with the idea that perhaps it was a good day for him to meet Christopher's parents as the man their son was dating, as opposed to the social worker they met at Watermeadow. Jason was feeling rather uneasy about meeting them, despite Christopher's constant reassurance that his parents were onboard. On some level, he wondered how he'd feel if it had been *his* son who'd been a patient at Watermeadow. Would he welcome his son's lover with open arms? He wrestled with the answer to that question, thus, he remained nervous about meeting them. Nevertheless, he suggested to Christopher that he see if his parents were available for lunch.

Wasting no time, the lunch date was immediately confirmed to take place at Christopher's parents' home. Jason's anxiety level only intensified as a result, but he knew it was a natural evolution in dating relationships, that at some point, you need to meet the parents.

Christopher offered to do the driving over to his parents.' While he was driving, he reached over with his hand to hold onto Jason's hand. "Stop worrying, honey. I promise you, my parents are cool with me dating you." He contemplated, "All those years I felt—alone, and afraid of confronting my father with the truth about myself. It's sort of surreal." Unfortunately, his words seemed to do little to ease Jason's concerns.

"Listen, whenever I felt like you're feeling now, you told me to take some deep breaths. So, go on, take some." Christopher began taking deep breaths himself to encourage Jason to do the same. He complied. After two minutes of this deep breathing exercise, his tension started to ease.

"I should have taken one of your Xanax pills."

"I did offer you one," Christopher reminded him.

Jason teased, "I guess we've come full circle. Now you're the social worker and I'm the patient?" As the car pulled into Christopher's parents' driveway, Jason gasped in amazement. Their home was enormous as well as ostentatious. He was not expecting their house to look like this. "Sweetheart, you didn't tell me that your parents lived in a mansion."

"I'm not sure if this really qualifies as a mansion."

"Considering the plain, modest home I was raised in, take my word for it. It's a fucking mansion! And the way it sits so far back from the road, it's more like an estate."

Still concerned about Jason's mental status, "How are you feeling now? Any less nervous?"

"Shit! Now it's worse. I've never met people this rich before."

"They're just people. Rich people have problems and heartaches just the same as poor people. By the way, my brother Jeremy will be here too. I'm not sure whether you ever met him at Watermeadow. He came to visit a few times."

"I don't think I ever did. More family to meet. My anxiety level just peaked!"

"There's nothing to be concerned about, I swear to you. Calm down and stop worrying."

The car came to a stop as Christopher parked at the end of what seemed like an endless driveway. "Sweetheart, look at me. I love you more than all the riches in the world. Nothing matters to me but you."

Putting on a cheeky grin, "Yes, you're right. Let's go. It *was* my idea after all."

Jason pressed the doorbell only to hear what was more of a melody playing than a simple ding-dong. "I've never heard a doorbell do that before." Christopher just smiled back at him.

Nate Parker opened the door. "Come in, boys, come in." He shook Jason's hand to greet him, "Very nice to meet you. Although I know this isn't the first time."

"No—I suppose not," Jason answered with a slight catch in his voice.

"I'm so glad it's under much better circumstances," Nate said feeling extremely grateful.

Jason put on a deliberate smile, "That's true. Much better circumstances than before."

Nate continued, "Just to let you know upfront, you've nothing to be nervous about." Jason's face glazed over with total surprise. "Christopher gave me a heads up on how nervous you were about meeting us."

Jason immediately looked at Christopher with shock, "I can't believe you told your father that."

"I wanted my parents to go easy on you, *and* I wanted them to make you feel completely welcome."

Jason sighed with some relief, "Thank you. That was very thoughtful." Turning his attention back to Nate, "Mr. Parker, your home is beautiful. I can certainly see where your son gets his good taste from."

"I think the word you're really searching for is where he gets his *expensive* taste from."

Jason laughed, "I'm glad you said it and not me."

"I know my son is just a *little* spoiled, but I guess I can take some of the blame for that."

Christopher feeling somewhat offended, "Uh—hello—I'm still standing here. You two are talking about me like I'm not present."

Nate pulled his son into a warm hug and gave the top of his head a vigorous rub. "I said a *little* spoiled," holding on just a little tighter. It warmed Jason's heart to see that kind of affection between a father and son, something which, during his lifetime, he hadn't had the blessing to experience.

"My wife and I owe you a giant 'thank you' for giving us back our son. We can't get over how well he's done and how good he looks. Not to mention how much he gushes on and on about you; Jason this and Jason that. I'm telling you, this boy has gone bonkers over you. Would it be all right if I gave you a hug too?"

"Sure, that's just fine." Nate hugged Jason with just as much feeling.

Jeremy came bolting into the foyer to greet the boyfriend he'd been hearing so much about. "Honey, this is my younger brother, Jeremy."

"Hello." Jeremy extended his hand for an energetic handshake. "It's a real pleasure to meet you at last. So, you're the guy who's been shagging my big brother," he said in a lighthearted fashion.

"Jeremy Parker!" his father cried out. "Have you no manners! You've embarrassed both me and Christopher, not to mention our guest." Nate turned to Jason, "I'm terribly sorry for my younger son's comments."

Although now Jason's coloring had slanted towards crimson red, "It's okay. I'm quite certain he meant no harm."

"Not at all," Jeremy said. "I was just trying to… To break the ice."

"That's how you break the ice? By humiliating me," Nate scolded.

Maggie arrived now to offer her welcome to Jason. "Sorry, I've been slaving away in the kitchen trying to prepare a nice lunch for us."

She just went ahead and gave Jason a hug. She felt no reason to ask for permission. "So, *you* are the new beau our son keeps talking about."

"Yes. That would be me. I was telling your husband how lovely your home is. It looks magnificent on the outside."

"Would you like a tour of the inside?"

Jason said with great eagerness, "Yes, I'd love that!"

Maggie smiled and gestured with her arm in a sweeping motion, "Well, come on then, I'll show you around." She escorted him on the grand tour of the Parker palace.

The two boys were back in Christopher's apartment napping after the delicious lunch Maggie had prepared. Now Jason could see where Christopher inherited his talent for cooking. His anxiety had completely vanished from all the warmth and kindness the Parkers had shown him. He couldn't get over how incredibly down-to-earth they were.

A knock on the front door surprised them both. "Who could that be I wonder?" Christopher asked. They both dragged themselves from bed to see who the unexpected visitor was.

Upon opening the door, "Jeremy, what a surprise? What brings you here," Christopher greeted.

"Sorry, I guess I should've called first. I hope I'm not interrupting anything."

"No, you're fine," Jason said.

"Remember the picture I took of you guys, right before you left the house. You know, so I could post it on Facebook."

"Yeah, what about it," his brother asked.

"I thought each of you looked fantastic in the picture! So, I ran over to the drug store to have it printed, and I framed it for you guys."

Jeremy reached into a bag and pulled out the box containing it. "Here, take a look. I made one for Mom and Dad as well."

Christopher opened up the box and slipped the framed portrait out. "Wow, you're not kidding! Look at this, honey. It's an extraordinary shot of us."

Jason took a close look at the portrait, "I see what you mean. We look like it came from a professional photo shoot where the photographer took a hundred pictures just for *the one* flawless shot. And those green eyes of yours, they look amazing."

"Everybody loves my brother's green eyes," Jeremy spoke with a tinge of jealousy.

Jason looked right into Jeremy's eyes. "I see, you didn't get the green eyes."

"Nope, I didn't. Just plain-old brown eyes."

"No, not plain, they're a rich brown color," Jason commented.

Christopher gave his younger brother a hug, "Thank you. That was sweet of you."

"You guys are welcome. Hey, Jason, I'm so sorry if I made fun of you guys with that *shagging* comment. I was just playing around."

Trying to ease his concerns, Jason spoke, laughing, "I knew that. I'm afraid your father was rather put off by it though."

Jeremy had a deep sigh, "I guess my big brother got his wish, after all."

"Um—what wish?" Christopher asked.

"Don't you remember that day in the courtyard at Watermeadow. What you said you wanted to do to Jason."

"Geesh, what in the world did I say about him?" Christopher was at a complete loss.

"You mean you can't remember?" Jeremy asked.

Christopher hunched his shoulders up, "I know I talked a lot about him, but I don't know what you're referring to." His brother leaned over to whisper in his ears, nodding with confirmation, "Now, I remember!"

"Let me in on it; what did you say?" Jason was burning with curiosity.

"This isn't going to make me look good, considering I was in rehab."

"That's all in the past. Go on now, what did you say about me?"

With hesitation, "I said that—I wanted to get into your pants."

Jason baffled in disbelief, "You *actually* told your brother that?"

"Not just my brother, but Susan too. I'm a little ashamed I told them but… I thought you were really hot."

Jason said to Jeremy, "He definitely got his wish." He gave Christopher a quick kiss.

Jeremy replied to Jason, "You guys look so happy together. You seem like a wonderful guy,"

"He is," Christopher said.

"I'll get out of here and let you guys have your privacy."

"Please, why don't you stay for a while. We'll probably just watch some television. Hang out with us," Christopher asked.

"Sure, sounds like fun." He paused. "But, are you sure? I really don't want to interrupt you guys, if you know what I mean."

Jason laughed, "Please stay. I promise we'll keep it G-rated. I assume two guys cuddling doesn't bother you."

Jeremy animated with a reassuring gesture, "Nah. Not at all. You've seen what they're putting on television these days?"

CHAPTER TWENTY-SEVEN
Late Saturday Night

It was late on Saturday when Jeremy decided it was time to call it a night. He'd greatly enjoyed the time he spent with his brother and Jason, but exhaustion was setting in. So, he said his goodbyes and left to go back home.

"I'm ready to collapse too." Jason asked Christopher, "How are you feeling?"

"Absolutely exhausted. I'm done for the night. Let's just crawl in bed."

Despite the evening's cooler temperatures, the two men shed every piece of clothing. They figured with a good snuggle, they could generate their own heat for comfort. Under the covers, Christopher was lying flat on his back, while Jason placed his head on top of his upper chest, pressing his face into the chest hair he loved so much. Like a kitten curling up in a soft blanket, he was running his fingers through the plush carpet of hair.

Being that both Christopher and Jason loved this position, they would take turns in bed as to who would lie flat and who performed the sensual body exploration. But for now, it was Christopher's turn to be the victim of Jason's wandering fingertips. Jason was enchanted with providing this kind of soothing and erotic affection. His roaming hand caressed Christopher's hairy legs and ball sack, and then traced his fingers slightly northward to stop and linger in place. Once nestled inside the region of dark pubic hair, his fingers moved gently around, but remained as if his fingers had become entrapped there. Christopher always enjoyed the stopover in what was his most favorite erogenous zone. Since body hair was such a huge sexual turn on for Jason, something about being entangled within such close proximity of Christopher's penis, would double his enjoyment. Christopher, being on the receiving side of this equation, would slip into a dreamlike state of sexual enjoyment combined with intense relaxation. Jason had also made the discovery, that the longer he lingered his fingertips in Christopher's pubic hair, would exponentially increase his chances of Christopher producing a massive, firm erection. Once he got Christopher hard, it would promote a level of seduction within himself, forcing his own dick to rapidly engorge with blood.

"I thought you were exhausted?" Christopher commented.

"I am, but I can't help myself! Your body turns me on too much. I haven't had an orgasm for several days. I've been saving myself for this weekend. Besides, you said you were tired too. You're just as rock hard as me. What's your excuse?"

"I'm currently being seduced by the man who I'm madly in love with. And your fingers seem to be pressing all the right buttons."

Jason, having no desire to pass on the opportunity to take advantage of Christopher's engorged, blood-filled penis, reached over to the nightstand to pull out a bottle of his favorite lube. He'd placed it there for easy access. Jason then peeled the covers down, revealing all the magnificent beauty that was Christopher's body. Jason wasted no time on latching his lips around the head of Christopher's cock, taking the entire length in his mouth and sliding all the way down till his nose became buried in his thick patch of pubic hair. Jason sucked continually in a slow but deliberate pace. During his sucking action, he used his hand to gently massage the region below Christopher's balls, with the desired effect of stimulating his prostate. This added massage seemed to always produce an additional mushrooming of the cock-head that Jason could feel with his tongue.

Opening the bottle of lubricant, he spilled an amount onto his palm. The lube was slathered over Christopher's throbbing member from tip to base. Jason made certain that the rigid shaft was lubed generously. He then climbed on top of Christopher, taking hold of his erection and gently easing his ass down over it. Allowing the lubricant to gently ease Christopher into his opening. Jason slowly, carefully sat deeper and deeper until Christopher's cock was deep inside him.

Christopher began moaning out his pleasure while running his fingertips through Jason's chest hair. He paid close attention to softly pinching his nipples, making certain that none of the stimulation could be perceived as painful. Jason very much enjoyed this sort of teasing stimulation of his nipples, but pain offered zero enjoyment. Both men felt it was important to do everything possible to heighten their partner's pleasure while being conscious of not doing anything that could be perceived as a negative. Not that being aware of each other's likes and dislikes was a hassle. Not at all. It simply wrapped their sexual activity in a blanket of romance that a quick, easy hookup could never do.

As Christopher's penis began massaging his prostate, Jason's cock began leaking streams of viscous precum, spilling on to Christopher's abdomen. Seeing this visual cue of Jason's pleasure, Christopher was driven ever closer to his climax. It was impossible for his excitement not to elevate from what his eyes conveyed. The warmth and tightness of Jason's ass sent him even closer to the point of no return. "Stop—please," Christopher asked Jason. With his request, Jason ceased his endless grinding of his dick. "I'm getting too close to coming." Jason leaned his body down so they could press their chests together as well as their lips. Being ever careful not to harm Christopher's firm dick buried inside.

Christopher reached around Jason to cup his hands round his ass. He sensuously caressed that amazing ass Jason possessed. And being that his ass was also generously covered in hair, it gave Christopher a higher level of tactile pleasure. It made him wild with desire. He nudged Jason's ass to signal he could restart his humping action. "Not too fast, honey," he begged. "Keep it slow. I want to enjoy being inside you for as long as possible. I can feel myself leaking inside you already." Jason sat up so Christopher could begin stroking Jason's erection while his own dick was being ridden. This added attention to Jason's hard-on along with the persistent stimulation to his prostate was simply too much, and it sent him over the edge. Jason's cock began spasming involuntarily, and his orgasm followed. His ejaculation shot over Christopher's chest.

Once Jason hit climax in this position, Christopher's orgasm was inevitable and nothing he could do at this point could halt it. Jason's prostate quivered like a vibrator on Christopher's cock, and his ejaculation erupted from the added stimulation. Christopher's face and moaning alerted Jason that he also climaxed inside of him. "Oh, honey, I'm sorry," said Jason.

Breathlessly he said, "You've nothing to apologize for. Stay still. Just let me stay inside you a little longer." Even if Christopher's orgasm had passed, he still wanted to enjoy this intense close intimacy they experienced. "Okay," Jason whispered back while bringing their chests together again.

After a minute or so passed, Christopher's erection had subsided to the point he couldn't remain inside any longer. As soon as Jason detected this, he climbed off and grabbed a white washcloth from the nightstand drawer to sponge away the evidence of their lovemaking, once again.

"That was fucking fantastic," Christopher said to Jason. "Damn! You're one hell of a lay!"

Jason grinned, "Like I always say, it feels nice to be appreciated. I'm crazy about having you inside me as well. But have you ever wondered why in movies and television, there's never any cleanup afterwards? It always looks so unrealistic to me."

"Well, I suppose it would make a scene that much more graphic. You should only have a visual of the humping without the sticky residue." They both laughed over that remark.

Jason climbed back into bed and started snuggling with Christopher again.

"Okay, now you lay on your back, so I can have a turn," ordered Christopher.

"With pleasure. I can't think of a better way to fall asleep." Just before Jason fell into a deep slumber, he told Christopher one last time, "I love you."

"I love you too. I love you too."

CHAPTER TWENTY-EIGHT
Facing Fears

Monday arrived, even if the desire for a three-day week-end was etched in Christopher's mind, Monday simply came too fast and for two reasons. Number one, he was already missing Jason's company, and number two, more importantly, he knew he had to confront Mr. Branson about who he wanted to bring as his date to the Employee Appreciation Dinner. He had managed to completely absolve his mind of that issue, since he was distracted with all the events that took place during the weekend. However, now the work week was upon him, he knew he simply had to tackle his fear of rejection.

His desk phone began ringing. "Good morning. This is Christopher Parker."

"It's just me, honey. Sorry, nobody special."

Immediately recognizing his boyfriend's voice, he replied, "You're *very* special to me."

"Thank you. I suppose that wasn't the best choice of words. I just meant I'm not somebody important like a client."

"I knew what you meant. But you gave me an opportunity to say how special you are to me and you *are* important too."

"Is it any wonder why I'm so in love with you?"

"Not to me. I'm clearly the best catch you have ever reeled in," said Christopher trying to be cute.

"And you're so humble to boot," Jason said sarcastically. "You seemed rather distant this morning before you left for work. I was slightly concerned."

"Everything is fine, really. It's nothing you've done. You're right though, I was preoccupied. I'm just so apprehensive about talking with Mr. Branson about bringing you to that dinner."

"Oh, that's all? Okay, well, let me put my social worker hat on for you." Addressing by his surname to help break Christopher's tension, "Mr. Parker, you seem to have yourself stuck in a certain mindset. You don't seem to realize that you have painted yourself into a corner. My best suggestion I can offer to you is to simply assume that anyone you meet will accept you totally and unconditionally for who you are. In other words, stop assuming the worst possible scenario. Now is everyone going to accept you as you are in this world? More than likely, no. But I think you'll be surprised to learn that there are many more people than you think who will accept you just as you are. Am I making any sense?"

"Yes, you are. I get what you're saying. I need to stop playing by the rules of someone else's game."

"Yes—you do. Homosexual men and women have been trying to play by the rules set by the predominantly heterosexual world we all live in. I'm not saying you shouldn't worry about your safety if your gut tells you to. Oh, sorry, honey, I need to go, a patient is here."

"Okay, bye. Thanks for calling."

Knocking on Mr. Branson's office door, Christopher tried to put on a brave front. "Come in," was heard. "Good morning, Christopher. Something I can help you with?"

"No. Not... Not exactly."

Mr. Branson asked, trying to use humor, "Then what *exactly* do you need?"

"It's about the Employee Appreciation Dinner."

"And... What about it?"

Christopher took a deep breath, "Um—you see—it's about the date I want to bring."

"Yes, your girlfriend, I remember."

Taking in another deep breath and then letting it out slowly. Mr. Branson then asked, "You seem like you're a little nervous. Why? This is meant to be a fun thing I enjoy doing for my employees."

"I *am* nervous, Mr. Branson. The dinner sounds like an exciting time, and I very much want to come. It's just that—you seem to have assumed I have a girlfriend. I do have a significant other. Someone who means the world to me, but you see..."

Mr. Branson cut him off before he could complete the sentence, "Oh, I see." He paused a moment. "I owe you an enormous apology. Of all people, I should have known better. I'm terribly, terribly sorry, Christopher. Please forgive me. You would like to bring your *boyfriend*. Is that what you wanted to say?"

Sighing with relief, "Yes, that's it. I've been fretting about how you might feel if you knew the truth."

Mr. Branson said in an emphatic voice, "Oh, you mean the truth that you're a human being like everyone else. A person who's entitled to the same level of respect, common decency, and both civil and human rights as any other citizen of our nation. And all you were hoping for was to bring your boyfriend to the dinner. Is that the *truth* you were worried about?"

To sum it up in a single word, Christopher was *gobsmacked*. Consternation camouflaged his entire face like a chameleon. Not in a million years would he have ever expected that kind of response. And he didn't quite know how to respond other than, "Uhhh—yes."

Mr. Branson deliberately smiled, "What's your boyfriend's name?"

"Jason Calhoun, sir. He's a social worker who specializes in chemical dependency."

"Just do me a small favor and tell Jason that I'm especially looking forward to meeting him. Can you do that for me?"

"Yes, sir. I most certainly will."

"Your being gay is not a problem for me, nor should it be for anyone on my staff. And if someone has a problem with it, they will have me to answer to. But honestly, I don't think any of the staff here will be worried. Look—I would like to tell you every company in the world shares my opinion. But you'd immediately know that I was full of shit! Prejudice or discrimination of any kind isn't tolerated here. I hope you're feeling less nervous now?"

"Much, much better. Thanks for your understanding."

"You're more than welcome." Just then, Mr. Branson felt he should confide. "Listen—there's a reason why I sound so..." Mr. Branson paused trying to think of a good word, "... impassioned. I have three children, two girls and one boy. Nick, he's my youngest. He's seventeen-years old and a senior in high school. Nick is gay. Now you know why I feel so bad for assuming you have a girlfriend."

"Of course, I completely understand now. But assuming I have a girlfriend isn't exactly a crime, so I wouldn't beat yourself up over it. After all, I shouldn't have assumed you might have a problem with me. That's just an issue I have, and I need to stop fearing rejection. Obviously, I have empathy for your concerns facing the gay community."

"Like so many fathers, I wanted a boy something awful. So, you can guess, after two daughters, how happy I was that we were expecting a boy."

"That must have been very exciting for you."

"Tremendously." After a brief pause, "My wife and I had our suspicions that Nick might be gay when he was young. Of course, we wanted him to come to us about it. At least when he felt comfortable enough, we did the best we could to let him know he wouldn't be rejected. That he should feel safe and comfortable in his own home."

"Apparently, you and your wife were successful," Christopher complimented.

"Yes. I suppose you're right. He told us he was gay about two years ago. We didn't care, it was never an issue for us. All I wanted was a son. Fortunately, I got my wish. But—with all that said—it's still hard as a parent to be fearful about their own child suffering discrimination at the hands of ignorant people."

Christopher was swept away by this insight, that in his entire life, this never crossed his mind. Not once. "I see. I've never thought of it from the perspective of being a parent. I'm sure you and your wife have shared those concerns. And the truth being the truth, your fears are founded. I'd like to be able to say otherwise, but then you'd know right away that I was full of shit." That comment broke the tension from this conversation and had Mr. Branson laughing. "You're doing a wonderful thing for Nick."

"I am? What am I doing that's so right?" Mr. Branson asked with a puzzled tone.

"You have given Nick total, unconditional acceptance. That's a *wonderful* thing! Trust me, sir. It's huge."

Mr. Branson sighed, "Isn't that my job as a father?"

"Yes, it is. Regrettably, many parents fail. I apologize if I sound blunt. There are a lot of individuals in this crazy world who don't have half your sense. And I understand why you're afraid for Nick. I wish I had a magic spell to remove those worries from your mind, but of course that's unrealistic. Look on the bright side though. The world is getting better. A whole lot better than it was for me. And it's already enormously better than it was for you growing up."

"True, life has become significantly better for the gay community. But it ain't perfect. So, at the very least, I can try to make it the best I can for you, as one of my employees," Mr. Branson exuded sincerity and graciousness.

"And it's very much appreciated," Christopher said.

"Thank you for sharing your truth with me. If my son could grow up and be as successful and competent as you, I'd be thrilled. Now, you better get back to work. That project you're working on for me is critical. I need those numbers badly, please. I want to be able to meet with our client this week."

"Sure thing. I'll get straight back to work." He exited Mr. Branson's office, brimming with good feelings and back to the task at hand.

CHAPTER TWENTY-NINE
Employee Appreciation Dinner

The weeks flew by, and the date for the once-feared Annual Employee Appreciation Dinner arrived. It was the first time either one of them had been to the prestigious Applewood Country Club. Jason and Christopher were looking forward to this event, and being that it was Friday evening, made for a great kick-off to the weekend.

Christopher was particularly thrilled to attend, as it would give him the opportunity to introduce everyone to Jason. For what was a complete mystery to Jason, he had gone from one extreme to another. Now Jason had become his trophy. Christopher had always heard of men talking about their trophy wives, so he thought he should be allowed a trophy boyfriend.

"What has happened to you?" asked Jason. "Three weeks ago, you were afraid of bringing me to this affair. Now you can't wait to put me on display. What on earth happened to my 'other Christopher'?" He was slightly uneasy and not sure he was entirely happy about being considered a 'trophy.'

"First of all, I always wanted to bring you to this dinner. I was simply afraid of what Mr. Branson's reaction might be. So, I worked up my courage because it was so important that you attend with me."

"I apologize, you're right. That's how it went down. Even so, I'm uncomfortable being a showpiece."

"Sweetheart, what's so wrong about me being proud of who I'm dating?"

"No, there's nothing exactly wrong with being proud of one's mate. Seems like a legitimate thing to take pride in. Yes, I get that." Jason paused a moment, "Honey, I love you, but let's be honest. You have a proclivity to expensive taste. And it's not as if you won me in an auction because you had the highest bid. Being considered your 'trophy' can be taken too far as well! I'm not some inanimate object to be toted around."

"Would you have preferred me to be the 'other Christopher,' instead? A man who is meek and fearful. Besides, I would think you'd be flattered by being the trophy. You know, the one that's always young and pretty."

Jason shook his head in disbelief because he had no argument for that. "Okay, you win. I can't banter my way out of your logic. You've got me beat." How could Jason deny this pleasure to the man he loved. Christopher was right. It wasn't a terrible thing to take some pride. Because above all, he knew this way of thinking was far more emotionally healthy for Christopher, especially when compared to him being afraid of telling Mr. Branson he had a boyfriend in the first place. He smiled with love in his heart, "You can show me off as much as you want. I'll just be the door prize you've won."

"Come on, sweetheart. Do you think I 'm going to treat you like you're not a real person?"

"No, I'm sure you won't," said Jason.

As the couple arrived, they were greeted by valets who parked Jason's car. The fact they had valets alerted the two men to just how upscale this evening would be. White-gloved doormen greeted and directed arriving guests to the appropriate dining room. The posh atmosphere gave them reassurance that they were, in fact, not overdressed for the occasion. Both men wore their absolute best, dark suits for the evening's affair.

The Applewood Country Club offered golf, tennis, swimming, as well as fine dining. The club facilities and banquet center had a décor, which felt Mediterranean in nature with colors that seemed to echo those of the sea. Additionally, Christopher noticed pastels of terracotta, yellow, and lavender. The archways and fireplaces were all classically rounded in shape. The furniture was composed of heavy, dark woods and highly textured, luxurious fabrics.

Upon arriving at the entrance to the banquet room for the dinner, they immediately noticed a table with a seating plan, indicating at which table each guest should be seated and place cards. They both scanned for their names on the plan. Christopher was the first to spot his, and then much to his surprise, found their place card read, '*Mr. Christopher Parker & Mr. Jason Calhoun.*' All the cards had been labeled with the names for each couple written in fine calligraphy. This shouldn't have been surprising, but the fact their names were written on a card together was an acknowledgment that they were indeed a couple as opposed to two bachelor men coming stag. Christopher was a person who paid attention to tiny details like this, which probably would've gone unnoticed by most, but he took note of it and understood the gravity of its significance. He took their place card to table five and sat it between two place settings to hold their spots. There was an open bar, and Jason went to fetch a couple of Cokes.

"Sweetheart, you know, I really don't mind if you want something alcoholic. I mean, I realize you don't want to drink in front of me, but it's really okay."

"I'm not much of a drinker, honey. Never have been. I'm a lot like George, just on rare occasions. Sometimes, I've gotten a beer with Peter. Don't forget what I told you about my father."

Christopher immediately empathized, "Oh sure, I can see how that might make you feel."

As the room began to fill up with Branson Software Engineering employees, along with their plus ones, both men couldn't help but notice that everyone was dressed to the nines. Many men wore tuxedos, and the women had on elaborate evening gowns made of silk chiffon or brightly colored taffeta, many adorned with sequins or rhinestones.

Coworkers all came over to say hello and chit chat. Christopher glowed with pride each time he introduced Jason to the people he worked with as well as their spouses or significant others. He flashed back to a time when he'd had such poor self-esteem. Working as a prostitute completely destroyed his self-worth. He knew back then, no one would've chosen him as a date, not being a common whore. Now, he was *somebody*. Somebody who actually mattered in this world. Somebody who was worthy of being loved. Somebody who was worthy of a magnificent, intelligent, and sexy-as-hell boyfriend like Jason. Yes, this was an affair of *somebodies*. And in Christopher's head — *everybody* who was a *somebody* — was in attendance.

Jason looked at Christopher, and his heart flooded with happiness. He was enchanted by watching his boyfriend's attitude as he ebbed with self-confidence. He remembered how Christopher was once consumed by shame. He understood why he abused alcohol to cope with his low self-esteem. Now, he smiled with the thought of how proud he was of him; that Christopher had come so far with his recovery. Most importantly, he was incredibly grateful, for having him in his life. Having a man who would love and cherish him. A man he'd gladly spend the rest of his life with. Jason had always felt the best things in this world were those that could be shared with someone you loved. He was desperately in love with this man.

Christopher noticed out of the corner of his eye, Mr. Branson and his wife, Elaine Branson, were on their way towards them. "Good evening, gentlemen. So, tell me, is this the Jason who makes you so happy?"

Christopher was blatantly beaming, "Yes, Mr. Branson. This is my boyfriend, Jason Calhoun." Jason firmly shook Mr. and Mrs. Branson's hands. Christopher continued, "He's smart, successful, loving, kind, fun to be with, and insanely cute! Every day I'm so thankful to have him in my life. His presence alone is enough to make me happy."

Mr. Branson blinked his eyes and twisted his head from side to side, "Wow! That's quite the introduction!" He asked Jason, "How do you maintain standing upright, with all those adoring adjectives being heaped on top of you?"

Jason laughed at this clever comment, "Quite honestly, he makes it very easy. I'm very proud of him and his accomplishments. If I'm ever feeling down, I just need to think of him, and I immediately feel much better."

Mr. Branson turned to his wife, "Darling, you need to take some lessons from Christopher here. I'd love it if you'd gush like that over me."

She just laughed, "I bet you would! You know, I must say, gentlemen, it's so nice to see two young people *that much* in love, and so supportive of each other! It gives me a source of hope for the future."

Christopher gazing over at Jason, "I agree. Love does seem to contribute to lighting the way towards a brighter future."

Mr. Branson asked, "Are you guys planning on getting married?"

The question caught them both off guard as Mr. and Mrs. Branson noticed the pointed pause. Jason began to stare into Christopher's eyes, seeming to get lost in the emerald pools. Grinning slightly, "I'd love to marry him someday. I want nothing more than to spend the rest of my life with him."

Mrs. Branson said, "Perhaps you might consider adding both of us to the invitation list. Wouldn't that be nice to attend?" she asked her husband.

Mr. Branson said, "We would be honored to attend your wedding. *Not* that we're rushing you guys. You two take all the time you need. On another topic, the Applewood Country Club has asked me to encourage my employees to wander around the club and take a self-guided tour. To be perfectly frank, they're hoping if you like what you see, it may encourage you to join the club yourselves. If you gentlemen would excuse us, they should be serving dinner very soon."

"Thank you for having us once again," Christopher said. "We're really enjoying ourselves."

"You're both very welcome."

The dinner was absolutely delicious. The service given by the Applewood staff was impeccable. Even though neither of the two men had any real intention of joining the club, it couldn't hurt to tour around it as Mr. Branson suggested.

Despite the late hour and the lack of sunlight, it wasn't difficult exploring the tennis courts, golf ranges, and the pools as the grounds and facilities were well lit. In particular, there was a stunning view from the rear of the main clubhouse building. It was perched high up on a hill and you could see the city lights sprawled out like a galaxy of stars. They both found the view breathtaking. "How would you like this for a backyard view?" Jason asked.

"It's so magnificent. Who wouldn't want to come home to this each night?"

"I can't dream of anybody who wouldn't. Let's get back to the dining room and say our goodnights."

"Sounds fine with me," said Christopher.

They walked back to enter the clubhouse at the rear entrance door. Upon opening the door, Christopher and Jason were abruptly startled as another gentleman and his wife were coming from the other direction to access the view the boys were returning from.

"Sam!" Christopher said startled. "What are you doing here?" As there was a woman present, he held his tongue. However, his gut wanted to shout expletives instead.

"We're members here," Sam Barron said in a curt tone.

"Oh, of course. Please accept my apologies," Christopher offered.

"Patsy, this is Nate Parker's oldest son, Christopher."

Despite the obvious discomfort of this chance meeting, he remained a gracious young man, "Nice to meet you, Mrs. Barron."

Sam Barron, now placing his eyes on the stranger to the left of Christopher, "And you are?"

"My name is Jason Calhoun. Very nice to meet you," he said knowing full well that was a bullshit lie. There was nothing nice about meeting him whatsoever.

Christopher cheerfully said, "Jason is my boyfriend. We're here for the Branson Software Engineering dinner."

"Oh—I see," Sam said with a jagged pause.

Sam Barron raised his eyebrows and graciously gave a nod with his head, "You gentlemen have a good evening."

On that note, Christopher and Jason hightailed it back inside to say their goodnights. Jason groaned, "Uhhh, that was most uncomfortable. I take it your parents still don't know the tawdry history you and Mr. Barron shared."

"Fuck no!" Christopher whispered as softly as possible. "Thank God, he's left me alone though! I'd nearly forgotten the man exists."

Mr. Branson spotted them entering the dining room, "Hello again. I wanted to catch you boys before you left home for the night. I have a personal favor to ask each of you."

Christopher answered, "Sure thing, what can we do for you?"

Mr. Branson went on, "Now, this is truly a personal favor I'm asking, and if you're not comfortable with it, I'll completely understand. Don't feel you have to say yes. I can assure you. If you're in any way uncomfortable, you are certainly welcome to tell me no, I promise this has no effect on your job."

Christopher somewhat concerned now, "Okay, well, I'm intensely interested in what this favor is that you want done, but a teensy bit scared also."

"I know, I sounded ominous, but it's just that I'm afraid I might be overstepping my boundaries with you as it pertains to an employer-employee relationship. Do you remember my son I spoke with you about?"

"Sure, I do. Your son Nick. He's seventeen-years-old, a senior in high school, and he told you he was gay two years ago."

Mr. Branson directed his attention over to Jason, "Well, I must say your boyfriend has a great memory!"

"Like an elephant, Mr. Branson. He has an uncanny memory."

"What about your son?" asked Christopher.

"You see, my wife and I are so impressed with how professional, kind, personable, successful, gracious, and gregarious you both are."

Christopher laughed, "Now who's piling on the adoring adjectives?"

Mr. Branson nodded in agreement, "But they're all accurate descriptions about you both. See, my wife and I were hoping that you both might spend some time with Nick. We felt it might be good for him to have some positive role models in his life. Perhaps role models you both wished you had growing up? We like the idea of him being mentored by a same-sex couple like yourselves. We want him to settle down with a nice boy someday. No parent wants to see their child grow up and be alone. I hope I'm making sense."

Jason answered, "You're making perfect sense. We can both understand how you're feeling. We'd be happy to do that for you. Wouldn't we, honey?"

Christopher smiled, "We'd be honored, Mr. Branson. Just give your son my phone number. We'll set something up with him. You feel certain your son will be receptive?"

"Absolutely! I'm quite confident. He needs to meet others from the gay community so he doesn't feel isolated. Thank you both so much for agreeing."

"Not a problem. Thank you again for dinner. You and your wife have a wonderful weekend."

"I'm glad you enjoyed the dinner. It was a particular pleasure meeting you, Jason. Good night."

They left the venue and drove to Jason's condominium for the night. Christopher said, "How nice that was of Mr. and Mrs. Branson wanting us to spend time with their son. It's nice to be validated like that!"

"I couldn't agree more. You have a terrific boss; you really lucked out on finding him."

Christopher emphatically said, "Most definitely!"

CHAPTER THIRTY
Nate Parker's Office

Spring weather was finally taking hold in the state of Indiana. Temperatures were mild again, keeping in the range of the fifties to sixties. Nate Parker's office was located in downtown Indianapolis, in a tall, all glass high-rise. His office was located on the twenty-seventh floor, which offered sweeping views of the city skyline.

Jeremy entered Nate's office, carrying a large manila envelope, "Here are those papers you asked me to pull together for you, Dad. The ones for Mr. Barron."

"Oh, thank you, Jeremy. I appreciate you doing this for me. Mr. Barron should be here soon to collect them; your timing couldn't be better."

Jeremy was a graduate of Purdue University with a Bachelor of Arts degree in communications. Nate's second son was sort of a lost puppy. Although he graduated from college the year before, he still didn't know what he wished to do for an occupation. So, being the doting father, he placed Jeremy on his payroll and gave him a job with his law firm until he found his place in the world. Jeremy essentially functioned as a paralegal.

Nate's administrative assistant, Rhonda, knocked on his office door, which was left ajar, "Mr. Barron is here to see you." Sam was standing right behind Rhonda.

"Come in, Sam. How are you doing today?" Rhonda closed the office door as she and Jeremy exited, giving the two men some privacy.

"Fine, thank you. I've been enjoying the spring weather," Sam said with great enthusiasm.

Nate handed Sam the large envelope of important documents, which he'd stopped by to retrieve.

"Thanks again for your help," Sam smiled.

"Always glad to be of service to you."

"That's a new picture I haven't seen in your office before," he said, noticing a framed portrait that was sitting on an adjacent bookcase.

"Oh—that—yes, it's a new picture my son Jeremy was kind enough to take for me and Maggie. Of course, you'd recognize Christopher, and the other gentleman is his boyfriend. They've been dating for quite some time now." He quickly felt uneasy and suspicious about Sam taking note of the picture, considering the level of hatred his son had for the man. "My son is gay in case you didn't know."

The sight of that portrait prompted a wave of jealousy to consume Sam, but he did all possible to prevent those feelings from being observed. Forcing himself to smile at Nate. "I did know that actually. I ran into Christopher and—uh—Jason, I think his name was, at the Applewood Country Club."

Nate was becoming increasingly uncomfortable now, "What were the boys doing at the club?"

Sam said in a snobbish tone, "One of our members, Jonathan Branson, was holding a dinner party where they were included."

Nate consciously remained cool despite the tone of Sam's voice. "That makes sense. Christopher works for Jonathan's software engineering firm." Feeling wholly uncomfortable, "If you'd be so kind as to excuse me. I have another appointment scheduled very shortly."

Every word in that sentence was a brazen lie. He wanted that man out of his office, but he had to employ the most diplomatic approach he could think of on the spot. The lie would serve its purpose.

Sam gave a nod, "Thank you for your hard work and service. Enjoy the rest of your day."

"You're more than welcome. Let's hope the weather remains this pleasant. You have a good day as well."

Sam left his office in a firestorm of concealed resentment. Nate, on the other hand, let out a huge sigh of relief.

CHAPTER THIRTY-ONE
Unwanted Visitor

Jason had just finished a counseling session with a patient who had a long history of drug abuse, namely, heroin addiction. He immediately began working on the mountain of routine paperwork that he always dreaded tackling.

Out of the corner of his eye, he noticed someone at his door. A visitor Jason wasn't at all happy to see. "Mr. Barron, what brings you to my office? I wasn't notified that you had an appointment with me."

Sam said, "Sorry, I didn't make an appointment."

"What can I do for you?" Jason clearly wasn't interested in engaging in conversation with this man.

"I'll come straight to the point. I want you to stop seeing Christopher Parker."

Jason, quite alarmed, "Excuse me! Why on earth should I stop seeing Christopher?"

"I've five-hundred-thousand dollars' worth of good reasons. That's exactly what I'll give you, five-hundred-thousand dollars. It's all yours. Just break it off with him. I know you're a man who has come from very modest means. I should think a half million dollars will come in handy."

"So, that's it! You think you can just buy me off?" Jason said with a voice, for which no one would mistake for anything other than outrage.

"You're going to drive a hard bargain then. Fine, I'll make it one-million dollars. Surely, becoming an instant millionaire should suffice."

Now absolutely outraged, "Who the fuck do you think I am? You couldn't buy me off with all the money in the world!" His anger was now mixed with tears, "I love that man more than life itself, and there is no amount of money that you could offer to extinguish my love for him. Mr. Barron, you can leave Watermeadow on your own, or I'll call security and have you dragged forcibly out of here. And trust me, if I call security, I'll see to it that you are banned from this facility permanently." With tears now pouring out of his eyes, "Do I make myself clear?"

"Crystal clear, Mr. Calhoun. But let me make something just as clear to you. If you have me banned from Watermeadow, I'll simply buy it. And once I do, you will be the first person on my list to terminate employment. I hope I've made my position clear too." Sam raised his voice, "End your relationship with Christopher, or I'll take whatever means necessary to see that you do." On that hateful note, he took his leave. He did not want to deal with the humiliation of being removed by security.

Jason was left in a state of complete and total shock. Without warning, he became short of breath, his heart rate increased, he had sweating and chills, abdominal pain, was pale in color, and had numbness from head to toe. He forced himself to leave the office and immediately spotted Nurse Judy.

"Oh, my God! What happened to you!" Judy shouted.

"Please, I need to get to the emergency room," he said, speaking through a shower of tears.

"Okay. It's the end of my shift. I'll take you myself."

"Thanks. Oh, would you call Christopher, please, tell him where we're going."

"Sure thing, sweetie. What's his number?"

"Here, just take my cell phone," he said while struggling to pull it out of his front pocket. "You'll find his number on speed-dial."

"Take a seat here," She pointed to a chair in the nurses' station. "I'm going to let the nursing manager know where you and I are going."

Jason sat down, "Thanks, you're an angel."

CHAPTER THIRTY-TWO
Emergency Room

Christopher frantically bolted through the automatic doors of the emergency department at Indianapolis North General Hospital. He'd raced over from work in a state of complete distress. He felt as if he was going to pieces, since he had absolutely no idea why Jason was taken there in the first place. What he did know was that Jason's coworker, Judy, had reached him by leaving a voice-mail on his cell phone and was bringing him in. He took some comfort in the fact that at least he wasn't being brought in by ambulance.

Thankfully, there was no line at the reception desk. He addressed the girl sitting at the window, "Excuse me, I'm trying to locate Jason Calhoun. He was brought in—I guess around an hour and a half ago."

"Yes, he's in room twelve." The receptionist pointed to some doors to the far-right side of the waiting room area. "I'll open those doors, and you can go on back. You should have no problem locating his room."

He thanked her and walked through the doors as instructed and easily found Jason's room. As soon as he saw Jason was still in one piece, *thank God*, he grabbed his face and kissed him.

"My God almighty! What's wrong. What happened to you?"

"I had a horrible panic attack. Judy was kind enough to bring me in."

"Thank you so much for looking after him," Christopher said to Judy.

"I was more than happy to do it. He's looking a whole lot better now. The ER physician ordered that an IV be started, and they pushed an intravenous form of Ativan through."

Christopher laughed a little, "Got to love Ativan! Seems to cure all that ails you." Taking in a deep breath to calm himself. "Sweetheart, you're not one prone to having panic attacks. What the hell happened?"

Judy intruded, "Not to interrupt you guys, but I'm exhausted. Since you're here now, Christopher, I'm going to take off. I've heard all I want to about that *unwanted* visitor. No doubt your boyfriend will take very good care of you."

Jason nodded, "You go ahead. I'll be just fine, and I'm sure I'll be back at work in the morning. Have a good night." She said goodnight as well and left for home.

"So, what's this about an unwanted visitor?" asked Christopher.

"That mother-fucking Sam Barron showed up at my office."

"That fucking son-of-a-bitch! Is it any wonder why I loathe that man so much?" He spoke with unbridled hostility.

Jason sneered, "Honestly, I'd like to push that arrogant asshole off a cliff. I swear to God I would! And believe me, once they heard my story, there isn't a jury that would convict me."

At that moment, Christopher collapsed into an available chair, "What did the jackass say this time?"

"He offered me one-million dollars to break up with you."

"He did what? Why would he pay you one-million dollars to break up with me? Does he think he can win me back? That man has gone off the deep end!"

"It just keeps getting worse. And I have to tell you, that man made me extremely apprehensive. He truly frightened me."

Shaking his head in despair, "Go on, what else did he threaten?"

"I said I wouldn't take his money and threatened to have him permanently banned from Watermeadow. He said he could easily buy the place. And once he did, he'd fire me. I believe him. This wasn't an idle threat. Sweetheart, I can't afford to lose this job. I've worked so hard to get where I am. Not to mention I need the money. If he took over Watermeadow and fired me, my career would be ruined. I can't take the risk." He welled up inside with emotion, "Nor do I want to live without you. I love you so much. I rather *die* than not have you in my life. What are we going to do? Please—tell me—what do you think we should do?"

Christopher reached over to grab Jason's hand and stared off into space. "Everything will be alright. Now I don't have a choice. I'm going to do what I should have done before. I'm going to tell my parents the whole repugnant story about Sam and me. My dad will know what to do. If there's one thing I've learned in my life, 'Father knows best.' You see, Sam Barron, the notorious handsome billionaire is one of my father's very best clients."

"Oh—my—fucking—God! You can't be serious?"

"Sweetheart, I love you. But I've never been more serious in my entire life." He hesitated, "One of my regular johns, also filthy rich, recommended me to Sam. Apparently, the guy showed him a picture of me, and, of course, he recognized me right away. That's how it all started."

The ER nurse, in charge of Jason's care, arrived in the room to let him know the doctor was ready to order his discharge.

"Thanks for your help. Brenda, is it?" Jason felt bad her name had momentarily slipped his mind.

"Yes, that's my name," she said.

"This is my boyfriend, Christopher. He's come to take me home."

Looking over towards this new visitor, "This is your boyfriend? That's not possible. No way this man could be your boyfriend."

Jason rolled his lips up into that cheeky grin, "I can definitely vouch for him, and why couldn't he be my boyfriend anyway?"

She turned her eyes back to her patient, "If I had a boyfriend who was *that beautiful*, there is no way I'd be having panic attacks! I'd be walking on air. This man is drop dead gorgeous!" Jason and Christopher burst out in laughter. Brenda gave a wink to Jason, "I'll be right back with your discharge papers."

"Sweetheart, would you like me to be there with you when you talk to your parents about that *monster*? I know this is going to be hard for you."

"Oh God, yes! You might have to bring me right back here with my own panic attack. I'm not looking forward to this. Not at all."

"You'll survive. If there is one thing I've picked up about your father—is that he wants to protect you. You know how much he loves you."

CHAPTER THIRTY-THREE
The Horrible Truth

The next evening, Jason drove himself and Christopher, over to the Parker's residence. He held onto Christopher's hand the whole drive over. Christopher was feeling queasy from anxiety. "Honey, I'll be with you the whole time," Jason said, trying to comfort him.

Finally, arriving at the door, Nate and Maggie greeted the boys. They suggested they should all sit and talk in the dining room. The two boys were on one side of the table, Nate and Maggie on the other side. Maggie also served some of her famous mint iced tea to both the boys.

"You sounded extremely upset on the phone," Nate said to Christopher. "So, what's going on?"

Christopher's eyes filled with tears and Jason reached over to rub his back, "You have to tell him, honey. I know how hard this is for you, but I'm here."

Christopher's nose started running, and he began to snivel. "I need to tell you guys the whole *sordid truth* about me and Sam Barron."

Nate Parker, very grateful that he could finally learn what the hell had gone on between those two, reached across the table to hold his son's hand. "Listen, Mr. Barron was in my office just the other day, and I have to tell you, I wanted to get rid of that man as fast as I could. He made me feel *extremely* uncomfortable. So, please, tell us, what happen between you two? We don't care how atrocious it is, honey, we're all here for you. So, out with it."

Using his sleeve to wipe away his tears, Christopher began, "It all started about five or six years ago…"

Nate and Maggie Parker looked as if someone had just told them their precious son had been hit by a train. Their faces were now tortured with grief, along with tears pouring down their cheeks. Nate, running a shaky hand through his hair, swallowed hard, "Oh, God in heaven, I wish you had come to us a long time ago. But considering the situation you had gotten yourself into, I can comprehend why you didn't want to tell us. It's not easy for your mother and me to hear that you resorted to prostitution. I suppose with your *handsome looks*, you were able to fetch an attractive price for yourself?" Nate asked half-joking.

For the first time ever, Christopher admitted, "Five-hundred dollars for an hour. Fifteen-hundred dollars for a day. Three-thousand dollars for an entire weekend."

Nate was flabbergasted, "So—*that's* how you did it. That's how you could afford your high rent and all the other luxuries you enjoyed."

"And as much alcohol as I wanted. Certainly, made more money than engineering ever paid." Christopher paused, "Looking back, it was so demeaning. My insides were torn up with the shame I carried with me."

Nate began choking up, "My poor son, selling his body to strangers. I had no idea the alcohol had you sinking so low." Nate was pale and in a state of disbelief. "Were you selling yourself to both men and women?"

"Just wealthy gay men. Sometimes I received offers from rich widows, who were lonely, but I always declined. I felt I simply wouldn't be able to achieve…," he had great difficult finishing the rest of his sentence. "…an erection. It's really embarrassing for me to even share something like that with you."

Nate reached over and squeezed Christopher's hand tightly. "No point in you being embarrassed. We're all adults here. And your mother and I aren't naive. You're a grown man, and you're certainly entitled to enjoy a healthy sex life." Nate's eyes suddenly became as wide as saucers, "What about AIDS? Or god knows what you might have picked up prostituting yourself. What if you passed something to Jason!"

Jason said to Nate, "Christopher is completely clean. So, you don't have to worry about that. Back, when he was in rehab, we had his blood tested for an entire panel of possible sexually transmitted infections. Every test was negative."

Nate let out a huge sigh of relief, and his eyes filled again with tears, "Praise God! He dodged a bullet."

Jason said to Nate and Maggie, "Yes, he did. He dodged a *big* bullet!" Turning his eye towards Christopher, "Your son was frightened to death of those blood test results. I hated scaring him like that. But when it comes to HIV, ignorance is *not* bliss."

Maggie said, "No, I agree. It's not." Her eyes filled with tears of happiness, "Oh, thank God. At least we have a shred of good news." She ran to the kitchen and brought back a box of facial tissues, which she sat in the middle of the dining room table. Maggie yanked out a good handful. "What are we going to do, Nate? Sam Barron is a monster. How are we going to stop him?"

"The word monster is too good for him!" said Nate. "He's a complete and total hypocrite! The man is gay, and he married that woman just for show! He hired a private detective to get pictures of Christopher in the act. How despicable and loathsome can one man be? Using those pictures for extortion; all to keep you with him as his personal sexual service. What a twisted son-of-a-bitch! And using bribery to break you both up! I just can't quite figure that out. You guys are right, he's gone off the deep end." He stopped talking for a moment and pondered. "Mr. Barron will have an unwanted visitor making an appearance at his office. I happen to know he's having a board of directors meeting tomorrow afternoon. I plan on gatecrashing it."

"Nate! Are you sure you want to do that?" asked Maggie.

"It will be my pleasure. That man doesn't scare me one bit. Not one bit! By the time I'm done with him, he'll be glad I'm not tearing him another asshole."

CHAPTER THIRTY-FOUR
Viatone Headquarters

The elevator arrived at the thirty-fourth floor of the world headquarters of Viatone. Nate Parker, dressed in a dark navy, pinstripe suit, along with a brightly colored red tie, stepped off the elevator wearing a pleasant smile. He was immediately inside the offices. Mr. Barron's receptionist, Phyllis, was behind the front desk.

"Good Morning, Phyllis. I take it Mr. Barron is in the boardroom at this time?"

She looked perplexed, "Yes, he is. How did you know?"

"Because. I'm his lawyer. I know everything."

Nate immediately began walking back towards the boardroom. She politely called out, "Mr. Parker, you can't go back there."

Shouting back, "Just watch me!" He burst through the boardroom door to find the board of directors meeting in progress. There was a long rectangular granite top table with Sam Barron sitting at the head and ten directors flanking each side of the table.

"Mr. Parker," Sam snapped. "What's the meaning of this? Interrupting our board meeting!"

Phyllis, having tailed Nate down the hall, "I'm terribly sorry about this, Mr. Barron. Mr. Parker walked right past me with complete disregard."

Sam reassured her, "It's okay, Phyllis. If you will excuse us." Looking directly at Nate, "Mr. Parker, I hope you have an excellent reason for this abrupt intrusion. This kind of behavior is uncharacteristic of you."

Taking a slightly disdainful tone, "That's correct; it is highly uncharacteristic for me; however, you and I have an extremely serious matter that needs to be discussed at once. This concern can't wait. I certainly have no qualms about disclosing the issues in front of your entire board. However, I somehow think you'd prefer to keep this confidential between you and me. The choice is yours. So, what's it going to be?"

Sam stood there, pursing his lips. "Very well, ladies and gentlemen, I beg your pardon, but we'll have to reschedule our meeting for another day. My apologies, but I need to ask you all to leave."

The twenty board members, although they were all whispering and grumbling, stood and exited as requested. The last one to leave was gracious enough to close the door behind her on the way out. Sam took a seat at the head of the table where he'd been standing. Tossing his hands into the air as a gesture of disgust, "You've got your wish. We're alone. Based on your obvious, deliberate, ill timing, I'm going to take a super-wild-ass guess this is concerning your son Christopher."

Nate, now wanting to grab Sam by the throat, and choke the life out of him, said, "You better fucking believe it's about Christopher, you spiteful asshole. Who the fuck do you think you are? Trying to sabotage the relationship, deliberately and maliciously, between Christopher and Jason. The word *anger* doesn't even do justice to how I feel right now." Trying to regain his composure, Nate walk to the head of the long conference table and took a seat that was adjacent to Sam. "You've got the entire world fooled, pretending you have a marriage and all the while you're as gay as a three-dollar bill. And trying to force my son into maintaining a relationship with you, when you're trying to hide who you are from the media. You were *using* him as your private sex slave. Dear God, almighty! Sam, you're twenty-two years his senior. What have you got to say for yourself?"

He said in a complacent tone, "I wasn't trying to use him as a sex slave. That's not fair. I'll admit, perhaps, sex was initially how it all got started."

"I'm so completely mortified my precious, first-born child had to turn to prostitution for survival in the first place. Do you have any concept of the horrific, emotional heartbreak it has been for me *and* Maggie?" Nate began shaking his head and tears began forming in his eyes, "I take some responsibility for my son's poor choices. I'll admit it! I didn't want a gay son. I've said and done some stupid, appalling things that derailed my son's successes. But the fact is, God gave me my son. I was an idiot to judge his good work." Nate turned his head to look Sam directly in the eyes, "Look at me!" Sam begrudgingly looked up from the blank stare he'd fixed to the top of the table. "I nearly lost my son in an ocean of alcohol, and you have more than your fair share of blame to take for that. Yes, you do. Controlling all the purse strings, just so he was *all yours*. You made sure you didn't have to share my son with anyone else! Jason rescued my son from what could have led to his death. Christopher, to a great extent, rescued himself from the brink as well. I thank God every day that he was bright enough to see his own death waiting for him on the horizon."

Nate tried to calm his emotions as much as he could, "Why? What on earth possessed you to go to Jason and threaten him like that? You scared him to death! He was rushed to the hospital with a horrific panic attack. I don't understand your actions. What was your goal?"

"Because—I'm still in love with him." He closed his eyes tightly, "I fell in love with your son, and I know there was a time he felt the same for me. I thought if I could remove Jason from the picture, perhaps I could win him back."

"You're a married man! You can't *have* my son! Whatever love my son had for you has simply gone, partly due to your actions. He's madly in love with someone else. And Jason is a good man. God chose my son to be gay, for whatever reasons, and I couldn't possibly ask for a more wonderful man for him. They deserve happiness together." Nate paused for a moment and laughed, "You know what's funny? My son didn't want to tell me what was happening between the two of you because of his good morals. The ethics and values I taught him. I've kept your dirty business secrets just like I have for many other clients. Every single time you created some fucked-up, corporate mess, I was paid to clean up after you. I was paid to bury all those dirty secrets, so nobody would know. And you paid my son for the use of his body, for his sexual services. Just so you had some outlet for your needs. In exchange, he vowed to keep your confidence, at any cost, so no one would ever find out who the real Sam Barron truly was. No matter how much I *pleaded* with him to tell me what was going on between the two of you, he wouldn't say. Christopher got those values from me." In his most hostile, sneering voice, Nate continued, "My loyalty to you is done! You leave my son and Jason alone. Because if you don't, I'll be the first one to talk to the media and tell them just exactly who and what you are. If you dare spill any of those *filthy pictures* you have of my son, I'll drag your good name through the deepest possible pile of shit. Let me tell you something. I've made my fortune already. I may not be as filthy rich as you, but I'm very comfortable. I don't care what happens to me or my name if I open my mouth to the media. Shit! I don't even fucking care if I'm disbarred." Repeating for emphasis, using one word at a time, "I—don't—care! So, you see, Sam, you won't hurt me, only yourself. What I do care about is my son, his happiness and future, and the man he wants to spend the rest of his life with. That's what matters to me! Have I made myself perfectly clear?"

Without warning, Sam broke down into a river of tears. Wailing and sobbing with the loudness and strength of a summer storm. Years upon years of pent-up feelings, exploding all at once, with the force of a volcano in a pyroclastic flow of raw emotions. Typically, this show of pure anguish would've normally softened Nate's demeanor, but it wasn't happening this time. He sat quietly waiting for the outpouring of emotions to calm down. Finally, as Sam began to simmer down a little, Nate asked, "Why on earth are you crying?"

Pulling himself up from the granite surface, he was crumpled over on, "I've hidden this—lie—for so long. Always trying to be something I'm not. I'm beyond exhausted from the constant hiding and deceit. Your son was this tiny, precious bit of sanity for me. When I was with him, he made me feel whole inside. So, I fell in love with him. I've hurt so many people along the way. Where do I begin? How do I right the wrongs of the past?"

Nate said, "That's easy. Does your wife know the truth?"

"God no! She doesn't," he said.

"Then start with her. Whether she'll keep quiet or not, I've no idea. But you need to do the same as my son had to. He made amends to all those individuals in his life he had wronged. What you wish to do about the continuation of your marriage is a question only you and Patsy can answer. If you want to lead the life of a gay man, which for you would be an honest life, then eventually the world will find out. Honestly, does it really matter? Why do you even care what people think? How does it really affect you? Other than your precious image."

Sam, in complete despair, said, "Where do I go from here?"

Demonstrating a modicum of pity, Nate said, "For the sake of my son…"

198

CHAPTER THIRTY-FIVE
Coffee Date with Friends

T he working week was over, and Christopher and Jason, after experiencing so much emotional upset, were meeting up with George and Susan for coffee at Starbucks. They wanted nothing more than to blur out Jason's panic attack, as well as all the heart-wrenching confessions Christopher made to his parents. The happiness they both received from the companionship of friends would greatly help tamp down their upset, if it wasn't possible to snuff out those memories permanently. But George and Susan were considered to be so much more than friends, they were family. The two boys had arrived about five minutes prior to the 10:30 in the morning meetup time.

Jason was standing in line for coffee when Susan and George strolled through the front doors. Christopher jumped up and gave a big kiss and hug to Susan and then leaped across to embrace George. "Jason and I have had such a dreadful week, you have no idea how happy I am to see you guys! You both look so wonderful. Being in love certainly looks good on both of you! Thank you, guys, for meeting us here."

Susan said cheerfully, "You're welcome! Where's your boyfriend?"

He used his head to nod over towards where Jason was standing at the cash register, "Right over there. Oh, here he comes now."

"Are you guys talking about me?" Jason said, greeting them happily. After placing the coffee on the table, he gave Susan a kiss on the cheek and grabbed George and gave him a tight squeeze. "As you can see, I already bought coffee for all four of us."

George smiled, "That was awfully good of you. You didn't have to do that."

Jason let out a big sigh, "Trust me, if you knew the hellish week we've had, you'd realize buying you both coffee is a small price to pay for your companionship. We're so glad to see you two."

Susan now worried, "That's what Christopher was telling us. Are you two alright? Would you like to talk about it? We're both great listeners, you know."

Christopher said softly, "Not today, but perhaps someday we will. The important thing is we're both just fine now. Couldn't be better and I'm still insanely in love with this man."

"There's no doubt you two are in love," George snickered. "The way Christopher brags about your sex life. Sounds more like a new form of gymnastics."

Jason said, blushing to Christopher, "Please, honey, you need to stop sharing the details of our sex life. That's meant to be between you and me."

"I'm sorry, sweetheart," Christopher said to Jason while wearing a mischievous grin. "But since the topic is out on the table," Christopher said to George, "Susan brags about your sex life, just as enthusiastically. I know more details then anyone has the right to know!" All four of them erupted into laughter.

Susan said, throwing her hands up, "What can I say, he's really good in bed."

Jason said, gesturing with his hands, "That's as much as we need to hear. If George makes you happy, that's all that's important."

Without warning, Christopher jumped, startled, as he felt some-one's hand resting on his right shoulder. Turning his head to see who it was, "Sam!" Susan and George's face washed over with disbelief, while Jason's smile became more of a scowl.

Sam said to Christopher, "I apologize for scaring you."

"How did you know where I was?" Christopher asked.

George leaned over to Susan and whispered in her ear, "Isn't that Sam Barron?"

Replying back in a whisper, "Yes, it is. I have no idea how he knows Christopher."

Sam continued, "I came here to apologize to you and Jason. Your father tipped me off that you'd be here this morning. He felt it would be best that I told you, how very, very sorry I am for my past behavior, in some place that was public. Your father didn't want you to feel threatened by me in any way. He also told me that I needed to make amends to the people I've wronged. After my wife, who of course hates me now, there is no one I needed to say how terribly sorry I am, than you. I know you probably won't believe me when I tell you I still love you, Christopher. But I realize you have Jason, and that's as it should be. I'm not asking for your forgiveness, because I can't expect you'd be able to offer it to me right now anyway. And I don't blame you." Sam turned his attention towards Jason, "I owe you a huge apology as well. I know how much in love you are with Christopher, and I had no right to try and sabotage what you two have. I also realize how grateful I am to you for rescuing him from his drinking. We all know where that would've ultimately landed him."

Christopher and Jason both had blank expressions. This revelation they were hearing from Sam was something their ears seemed to refuse to hear. Sam reached into his pants pocket and pulled out a USB flash drive and handed it to Christopher.

"What is this?" Christopher asked.

"Those are all the digital files of the pictures. You have my word that there are no copies of those files anywhere else. That flash drive is the only copy that exists now. As I've already said, you have my word on it. Perhaps one day, somewhere in the not too distant future, you will find it in your heart to forgive my actions. There is nothing more I can say, other than to beg your pardon for my interruption. I hope all of you enjoy the rest of your weekend."

Sam started heading towards the front doors, but Christopher yelled out to him, "Wait, Sam."

Sam turned to acknowledge him, "Yes?"

"Thank you. You're right, I'm not ready to forgive you just now, and I don't know if I ever will. But thank you all the same. You know, let me just share this with you. The single most important thing I learned during my rehabilitation and after was that I need to live an open and completely honest life. Otherwise, you start suffocating. Maybe the world isn't ready to accept the true you. That's their problem, not yours."

Sam smiled briefly, "Thank you." He turned and walked out of Starbuck's front doors, to whatever was to become of him, his life, and reputation.

George felt completely flabbergasted, "So, uh, how do you both know Sam Barron? And what on God's green earth was all that about?" He asked Christopher, "He said he loves you? And apparently tried to sabotage your relationship?"

Christopher sat down again with his friends. "Well, like we said, we had a hellish week! To be honest with you, guys, we really would prefer not to talk about it. It's a very private situation that we would rather not discuss. Just know that for Jason and me, we 'lived happily ever after!' Sam Barron happens to be one of my father's best clients. At least, he used to be. Not so sure about that now." Desperately wanting to change the subject, "On a happier note, we want to invite you over to my parents' house next Sunday. We're going to celebrate Jason's thirty-first birthday."

"Sounds like fun! We'll be happy to come," said Susan. "So, what would you like for your birthday," she asked Jason.

Jason smiled and gave Christopher a peck on the lips. "Trust me, I already have the best birthday present any man could ever ask for. Christopher is finally the one frog I found—who magically transformed into a prince."

CHAPTER THIRTY-SIX
Jason's Birthday Celebration

Nate and Maggie Parker weren't the kind of people to ever put up decorations. In light of trying to make Jason feel that he was part of the family, and to make his birthday a little more special, they did a modest job in trying to dress the family room with some streamers and one great big 'Happy Birthday' sign.

This was going to be just a small party with only the most important people in Christopher and Jason's lives. Jennifer, Peter, Susan, and George had already arrived. Jeremy was also present.

Jennifer asked Maggie, "Where are Jason and Christopher? We can't very well celebrate a birthday without the birthday boy."

"The boys had to stop to pick up a very special guest. That's all we know," Maggie said while gesturing with both hands in the air. "Apparently, they forgot to allow themselves a little more time." The familiar melody from the Parker's doorbell began chiming. "That must be them now." She asked Nate, "Honey, would you please get the door? Must be the boys."

"Sure thing," Nate shouted through the house as he walked to open the front door and much to his surprise, the special guest they heard about looked to be an older adolescent. "Hi, boys, please come in. And who's this handsome young man you have with you. Don't tell me you guys have started adopting strays off the street," Nate asked, trying to be cute.

"Hardly," Christopher said. "This is our new friend, Nick Branson. Well, actually, Nick is short for Nicholas."

"Nick Branson?" Nate said in a questioning tone. "Any relation to Jonathan Branson, young man?"

"Yes, Mr. Parker. He's my father," Nick said in the politest manner.

Nate held out his hand to shake. "It's my pleasure to meet you. We're very happy to have you at our home."

"Thanks so much, sir. Your house looks so cool. Looks gigantic from the outside," Nick said with enthusiasm.

"You think so, young man? Well, why don't you go ahead and have a look around. It looks just as gigantic on the inside I promise you."

"I can? Are you sure, Mr. Parker?"

"Absolutely! You go on. Enjoy yourself." So, with his permission, Nick took off to explore.

Nate smiled at Jason and Christopher, "Isn't he the politest young man?"

"He sure is," Christopher said.

Nate, who clearly was intrigued, asked, "Why do you two have the boss's son of all people?"

"Mr. Branson and his wife asked us, as a personal favor, if we would spend some time with Nick. He's just seventeen-years old, and he told his parents two years ago he was gay. They wanted their son to have some positive role models in his life, so he asked if we would share some of our time with him and act as mentors."

Nate beaming with pride, "That's quite a compliment to you guys!" Jason and Christopher gave a nod of agreement. "I suppose, in a peculiar twist of fate, the fact that you're gay, served as a hidden blessing to Jonathan Branson. I'd no idea his son was gay. Never mentioned it to me."

"This is actually only the second time we've been with him. But he was extremely happy the last time we saw him," Christopher said. "Mr. Branson was worried his son was feeling isolated. Which, unfortunately, was true; he was feeling that way. When we picked him up today, Mr. Branson was eternally grateful to us. He couldn't thank us enough. He told us how excited Nick was to come out with us today. And Nick is such a sweetheart; he's the perfect gentleman. He hasn't told any of his friends or classmates about his sexuality, yet. Which, still being in high school, Jason and I understand his concerns. High school can still be rough for gay teens. Unfortunately, he's dealt with some bullying already. It's been hard on him."

"Why is he being bullied if he hasn't told any of his peers he's gay?" Nate asked.

"You don't have to tell people, Dad. Most of us give off a certain vibe or demeanor. Kids are cruel. And they can be especially cruel if they think you're different in any way."

"Oh, I know what you're talking about now," Nate said. "Kids can be awfully cruel. A young person shouldn't have to go through that. Of all people, I should know. You boys are doing a wonderful thing for him! The kind of impact the two of you can have on his life. I can see why his parents are so tickled. Well, let's go join the others."

They all moved into the family room where the rest of the family and friends were waiting. Kisses and hugs were exchanged. They were all enjoying hors d'oeuvres along with happy conversation. Nick finally joined them in the family room after his exploration.

"Mr. Parker," Nick said to Christopher, trying to address him.

"Nick, remember, please just call me Christopher."

"Yes, Christopher, sorry. I've got to show you something."

"Okay, sure, but first, let me introduce you to our friends." After all the introductions were made, and everyone became instantly charmed with the young man's personality, Nick dragged Christopher and Jason to an upstairs bedroom, which for the life of them, they had no idea what he had seen that caught his attention.

Once the three of them entered the bedroom, Nick excitedly said, "Look at all these ribbons and trophies! I've never seen so many before. Who do all these belong to?"

Christopher said, trying to be humble, "They're all mine."

Nick's eyes opened even wider in enraptured amazement. "These are all yours? That's so cool! When did you win all these? You must have been super talented and smart."

Jason said, "He's right, honey. This is pretty impressive." Christopher didn't speak a word. His eyes scanned carefully all around the bedroom, allowing the vision of all those honors and accolades to be drunk in by his brain. It all seemed like a lifetime ago. As he would be twenty-eight-years old in several more weeks, his conscious brain told him that a lifetime ago was nothing more than hyperbole. All these achievements, once upon a time, meant so much to him, he smirked to himself, but not anymore. Just the image of Jason standing right next to him, reminded him of what accomplishments and achievements took precedence in his life. This moment, right here, right now, was the greatest gift anyone could possibly receive. Nothing else mattered.

Nick gave a little tug on his shirt, "Christopher, are you okay?"

He rapidly snapped back to reality from his dreamlike state, "Oops, sorry, I drifted away for a moment."

"I still can't believe these are all yours!" Nick glowed with astonishment. "You're so cool!"

Now being bashful, "Oh, I don't know about being all that cool. I'm just a regular guy."

Jason pressed his lips against Christopher's, "I think you're pretty cool myself."

"Okay, you two, let's get back to the rest of our guests before my head starts to swell."

☙

Everyone had enjoyed the lunch Maggie had prepared. Jason blew out thirty-one candles, which someone was outrageous enough to place on top of the cake. No one would man up and admit to doing it, though. The cake was exactly what he wanted, white cake covered in white icing. That flavor combination seemed a bit dull for Christopher's taste buds, but the day belonged to Jason. However, something about the simplicity of white cake with white icing sent Jason into a euphoric high.

Jason said, "This cake tastes incredible! It's my favorite. Thanks for getting this for me," he said to Maggie.

"Oh, please, you're more than welcome. Christopher told me this cake was your favorite kind. It's from Schlossmann's Bakery. I've always had good luck buying there."

"It's delicious! I'll definitely have to start going there myself."

Christopher gave a soft nudge to Jason, "Sweetheart, I got you a little birthday gift."

"Honey, I told you that you are all the birthday present I need. You really shouldn't have."

"I know that, but I wanted to just the same."

He shook his head back and forth, "Go on then, what'd you get me?"

Christopher stood up, and in the most typical, cliché way possible, collapsed to the floor on one knee, grabbed a small box from his back pocket, and flipped open the lid. Revealed to everyone in the dining room were two solid gold wedding bands. The rings, being highly polished, glistened under the light shining from the crystal chandelier hanging above them. The surrounding family and friends all seem to simultaneously gasp in awe and wonder. Immediately, Jason's heart was deluged with emotion as he knew exactly what was coming next.

Summoning all the courage he could, just to keep his composure, Christopher spoke, "Jason, I realize that this is a rhetorical question. Nevertheless, a question I still feel is important enough to ask. There is no one else in this world, who I'd rather spend the rest of my life with. No one else, I want to wake up each morning beside. No one else, who fills my life with as much joy and laughter as you. Will you please do me the honor of marrying me?"

Jason was overwhelmed with happiness, and his eyes filled with tears. Although he started hiding his face in both hands, he nodded up and down, to indicate his answer was yes. That wasn't quite good enough for Christopher's desires. "I can't quite hear you, sweetheart. What did you say?"

He tried to calm himself and pulled his hands away from his face, "Yes, my answer is yes. There's nothing more I would love than to marry you." Jason reached around Christopher's head and pulled his lips against his own. "For so many years, I was afraid I'd never meet the right guy, almost giving up all hope."

The room exploded in cheers and joyful congratulations. Peter, also in tears now, grabbed Jason, and hugged him as tight as he could, "I promised you Mr. Right was out there."

"Yes, you did," Jason said to Peter. "Thank you so much for always being there for me."

"I'm always going to be there for you. That'll never change. I love you, buddy."

Letting go of each other, Jason said, "I love you right back."

Nate and Maggie were elated for such a match for their son. She hugged each of the boys. Nate was glowing as he said to Jason, "Welcome to our family! Can't tell you how happy I am to have a soon-to-be son-in-law."

Jason gave Nate a hug. "I can't wait to have that title officially. I was just thinking, since I haven't had a father for such a long time, would it be alright with you if I just called you Dad from now on. Isn't that one of the son-in-law privileges?"

"Nothing would make me happier. I can't tell you how grateful I am for this moment. I'm incredibly grateful!"

"You have to promise to call me Mom, too," Maggie said as she hugged Jason.

"Sure thing, Mom." Jason paused, suddenly being pulled by a haunting thought. George snuck up from behind to steal a hug from Jason.

"Congratulations?" George said. "No one deserves this happiness more than you," he said as he embraced Jason tightly. "Can you believe it? You're actually getting married."

Releasing themselves from the tight hug, "So, I'm curious now. Since Christopher asked you to marry him, does that mean you have to take his name?"

"I don't think there are any hard and fast rules about names. I don't know, *Jason Parker*? Hmmm… Actually, I think I could get used to that. Hey, come with me." Jason took George by the hand and led him into the kitchen. "There's something I need to do, and I could really use your support."

"Sure thing, whatever you need," George said.

Jason realized that this engagement to his now future husband meant a new beginning in life. Perhaps, just perhaps, a fresh start would be just the thing his life needed. Stepping into the kitchen with George, he pulled his cell phone from his pants pocket. Jason dialed a number. George had no idea about who he was calling or why Jason wanted him to be by his side. The mystery number rang, and Jason reached over to hold George's hand.

"Hello," came an answer on the receiving end of the phone call.

"Hi—Mom—it's me, Jason. I'm getting married…"

THE END

About the Author

Eric Huffbind is a man of many talents. He's a hopeless romantic, licensed registered nurse, has been a travel agent, and is the eternal social butterfly. Among his passionate interests are history, genealogy, romance, and travel. Like so many other individuals, he has a long bucket list. On the list, to no surprise, was writing a novel. So, this, his debut novel, is a lifetime of raw emotions: be it love, happiness, sadness, tears, joy, anxiety, fear, disappointment, or achievement.

Although the story in this book focuses on the romantic relationship of two gay men, regardless of your sexual orientation, this novel is meant to rekindle the true spirit of romance and love in your heart. If Mr. Huffbind's story moves you through an array of emotions, and it touches your romantic spirit, please share the book with a friend.

Mr. Huffbind was born in Cincinnati, Ohio and has remained in southwest Ohio for his entire life. He shares his life with his husband, an autistic son, and his beautiful Pomeranian. He may be reached at **eric@erichuffbind.com**.

12437325R00125

Printed in Great Britain
by Amazon